Body on Ice

A VERMONT MURDER MYSTERY

✳

Based on a True Story

Alan S. Kessler

Softcover ISBN: 978-1-938394-85-0

Library of Congress Control Number: to come

Cover Art & Design: Baki Boquecosa

Layout Design: Grace Peirce

published by
Leviathan Books

Books by Alan S. Kessler

Novels

A Satan Carol
Shadowland
Clarence Olgibee
Gables Court
The Butcher
Ghost Dancer

Poetry

Damnation and Cotton Candy

1

Maybe their shadows and voices remained in the parlor, the ghostly remnants of a party forever floating like fog through time. The coy smile, the well-placed touch, the molasses smooth voices of men seducing giggling, gin fizz women, eternal foreplay forever trapped in this dark and silent house with clocks on every wall. When in their rooms, the lovers didn't think about ghosts, Hell, or even the very real consequences of lust. Their narrow beds creaked until stilled by finished desire, the only remaining sound the clocks' continuous ticking.

11:00 pm.

She got dressed and knowing her way down the darkened back steps of Mrs. Porter's home, walked quickly into the night.

On South Main Street in Stone Valley's South End, a two-block section of saloons and bordellos pitted by granite dust, dead trees lined a wooden walkway, fog on twisted branches hung like strips of torn shrouds. The planks unevenly spaced, mud and ice in the gaps, she worried about dirtying her new cloth shoes, a gift from her husband who, for her birthday, had also bought her expensive leather gloves. Two blocks from Mrs. Porter's, she stepped from the boards to the flagstone sidewalk of North Main Street's downtown and let her long skirt again dangle free.

Twenty-nine, slender and shapely, her large eyes as dark as her straight black hair piled high under a fur hat, she drew her cape closer against the cold and stayed in shadows. The stores closed, the Civic Council meeting over and the rest of the respectable part of town sleeping, her footsteps were the only sound as she continued toward home. Her husband might be there, she knew her children were asleep in their room, her father staying with them every Saturday night.

At the Bijou, the 8:35 showing of Tom Mix's movie, *Mr. Logan*, finishing two and half hours ago, she read the poster's catch line: Grim Duty Outweighs the Call of Love

She loved going to the picture shows.

A wagon of shouting, drunken, out-of-towners, some of them hanging over the sides, rolled past on their way to the next saloon. A man standing at the back jumped out, dashed to the sidewalk, and after twirling her around, laughed, then ran to catch up with his friends. Shaking, determined not to cry, she hurried on.

Blurred by the fog into a phantom vehicle with a shadowy driver, a motorcar, swerving between ruts made by wagon wheels and hard rubber tires, bounced along, slowed, keeping pace with her, then stopped.

She walked over.

"Tomorrow night, in the cemetery."

"I'll be there." He grabbed her arm, pressed his lips hard against hers.

"Someone is going to see us."

"Not if you get in."

Quickly crossing through the dim beams of light from the car's electric headlamps, she opened the passenger side door.

They drove up North Main Street, turned right onto Winter. She smiled knowing that tomorrow, before church, the pastor walking ahead of the family, she'd again secretly give her children candy. During the war, as a Red Cross volunteer making hospital dressings with other women in the basement of her husband's church, she worked ten-hour shifts, went home to wash clothes, cook dinner, read scripture to her three daughters, and before kissing them goodnight, made sure they knew how much she loved them.

Margaret, Ruth, and Marie, each a miracle, now only two blocks away, their rock candy in her pocket.

He stopped the car beside a large backyard surrounded by an old picket fence, this garden area, now frozen vines and rotted berries preserved in ice, as fog-covered as the house in front.

"I've got to get home."

"Me too," he answered, "but I have something fun for us to try."

In her skin, through her quickening heart, she again felt the thrill of sin. Any man would do, but this one was more interesting than those who barely controlled their lust. Imaginative and forceful, coldly efficient, he pleased her, the intense physical sensation adding to the liberating sweetness of infidelity. And tonight, he'd brought a rope.

He opened the gate and as they walked across the icy ground, she knew that in a few minutes she would wear a new wedding gown, one of blood and flesh. She'd be a bride reborn into the body of a woman no longer waiting for her husband's gentle touch.

They stopped. He tied her hands. She drifted backward into his arms, submitting to whatever he wanted, the choice hers.

A rope around her neck, the square knot in front pressing against her throat, a handkerchief looped over the knot, the cloth twisted from behind, pulled tight, twisted tighter—she couldn't scream, she could only kick—

Fighting him, struggling—

Then darkness.

He continued strangling her.

The man drove away. Face up, a death mask of fog clinging to her, she stared into the silence that follows violent death in lonely places.

Early next morning, Butch Pratt, 18, staying at the Arc Hotel, ran and stopped Deputy Grange walking his North Main Street beat and told him about the dead woman he'd seen from his window. They went to the yard, Pratt a few steps behind the police officer.

Grange carefully rolled the body over. Pupils fixed in mid-position, the mole below one eye black on pale waxy skin, she looked up at him.

"It's Rose." He quickly covered her with his coat.

Rose Thornton, the pastor's wife, Red Cross volunteer and Saturday night visitor to Nellie Porter's sporting house.

Wearing only shoes and tan gloves, her coat, hat, and cloak in one pile, blouse, skirt, petticoat, corset, and ripped knickers in another, everything neatly folded, she again lay face up on ice next to her empty purse.

"Remember not to sweat," Grange's mother reminded him.

An easy choice if you're not standing over the body of a dead woman.

Panting, sweating through his shirt, he ran to report the murder, knowing this sudden exertion would probably kill him.

Did I do something bad?

"Did you have another spell?" his mother answered, her face smiling at him through the fog.

2

On his early morning patrol through the North End's downtown, Leonard Grange would slowly walk the five blocks down one side of North Main, stop at the diner for coffee and a hot buttered roll, then crossing the street continue his leisurely beat, pausing to talk to the hardware store owner and Mabel at the town's telephone exchange.

Leaving downtown, he'd stroll up Winter, passing the Colton backyard where every spring Mrs. Colton and her grown daughter planted a garden, turn on Summer, the street of churches—Catholic, Methodist, Presbyterian, Congregational, Baptist, and Pastor Thornton's Stone Valley Church of Christ, the pastor and his family living in the small house next door.

At the Arc Hotel on the corner of Summer and Pearl, he'd head down Pearl to Jefferson, say hello to Mother Mae sitting guard duty on the porch of her boarding house for women. Back on Main Street, Grange would stop at the diner for a doughnut, the only place in town where they were sold. The cook bought them from the town baker, both having served in France during the war. The men remembered the beignets French women volunteers brought to the American soldiers in frontline trenches, the sweetened dough a reminder of home.

The cook never went to Fourth of July fireworks. The baker covered his ears whenever he heard thunder.

Instead of 36 minutes, the time a man walking at a normal pace would need to cover the eighteen blocks of Grange's patrol area, his morning rounds always took him twice as long.

For his afternoon patrol, he drove the police department's new

Ford Model T police truck, his route through the North End's two residential areas. In the one with Victorian and Gothic Revival homes owned by doctors, lawyers, owners of quarries, tool companies, and the railroads two branch lines, someone would occasionally nod at him or riding past in a four-wheel carriage, offer a curt good afternoon. Where the quarry workers lived, their houses neat Cape Cods or more modest dwellings—kitchen, two bedrooms, storage area— he'd stop and give candy to the children playing outside.

A soft rounded man with gray hair, bushy eyebrows and a thick mustache curling up toward sleepy blue eyes, Grange sat when he could, walked instead of running, and enjoyed the leisurely drives in his police truck. Because everything alive had a limited number of heartbeats, he didn't want to waste his, not even on Saturday nights in the South End.

But when nearing the granite mansion built on a hill in the center of the North End, its cantilevered gables, black towers, turrets, and massive chimneys casting a wide shadow over homes and the road, he felt an unnatural and unhealthy need to speed past. A woman he once loved had lived here.

A dark building, the only light visible from the street the candles downstairs and on the second floor where, at the end of a row of large leaden windows, feeble gaslight and shadowy flames streaked a small windowpane. Through this office window, Roscoe Perkins could be seen sitting by the fireplace. From here, he controlled the South Side, decided what to publish in his Stone Valley *Gazette,* and who to bribe. In a corner of the room his attendant, a seven-foot, voiceless man, watched and waited.

Grange would accelerate and when beyond the mansion, talk to his mother while driving slowly and enjoying the ride back to the station.

3

Monday Day One

His father had taught him how to track a bear with hounds or attract one with corn and rotted garbage. On another sober day, he educated him about turkey hunting and life.

"Although they've got pea-sized brains they're good at surviving so never hunt them with only one kind of call and when possible, go for a lone Tom who might be stupid enough to believe you're a hen. A good hunter understands how turkeys think. Some might attack if you're near the decoy. People are like that. You might be in the way of what they want. Just grab them by the neck and twist."

"There's a hard fact for you to know," his mother once told him while chopping wood. "Every jackass thinks it's a stallion. You're not a stallion but that don't mean you have to act like an ass." She lived until 80, died field dressing the wild hog she'd shot. Thirty years earlier, a bear turned and charging past the dogs, mauled his father who bled to death in the snow next to his whimpering hounds.

Sheriff Bull Gideon Jones understood his parents' lessons and why they had beaten him. Life required toughness. There were no lame or weak animals in the forest, only their bones. But he also had to be smart. Crimes, omissions, rumors, accidents and mistakes, had consequences. With humans, money bought power, and Roscoe Perkins had the sharpest claws in town. Over the years he'd become skilled at protecting himself by knowing exactly what to do to keep Perkins happy.

As big as his parents but more muscular, Jones had a wide face, bald head, small eyes, and hairy knuckles he liked to crack because the soothing sound reminded him of his childhood. He had added Bull to his name.

After Grange told him about the body, Jones realized if he didn't control the story its salacious nature would bring reporters to Stone Valley. At the Colton's, he ordered the crowd of gawkers pressing against the fence to leave, assigned two deputies to rope off the garden and stop anyone from getting within a block of the property. After telling Grange to take photographs of the yard and the tire tracks on Winter Street, he slowly walked the field.

When finished, Jones questioned Mrs. Colton and her daughter. Shocked, trembling, holding each other close, neither had heard anything, both sleeping peacefully while someone strangled Rose Thornton in their backyard. Her body on the way to the Quigly and Gack funeral home, he drove to the dead woman's home.

A church woman let him in.

"They're in the parlor."

Other members of the pastor's congregation were there. He could tell everyone knew.

Jones went quietly into the room.

Tall and thin, dressed in an unfashionable black frock suit, Pastor Chiles Thornton sat stiffly in his ball and claw armchair, his back not touching the leather. His graying hair cut very short made his broad forehead seem even bigger, cheekbones sharper, a pronounced jawline more severe. Certain of his knowledge of God's will and Satan's desires, he looked straight ahead, his dark eyes barely blinking, his lips pressed tightly together.

"Pastor," Jones said softly, waited until Thornton turned toward him. "I'm sorry about Mrs. Thornton."

"When may I see her?"

"Whenever you want. I'll place the call."

"I—I'll go too," Rose's father said, his voice trembling. He stood on the other side of the room, next to the children sitting silent and unmoving on a needle point loveseat.

"That won't be necessary, Henry," Thornton said firmly. "You're needed here."

Hands shaking, the old man took a faded bandanna from the pocket of his baggy pants held up by suspenders and wiped his eyes.

"How was she killed, Sheriff?" Thornton asked him.

"The girls should leave."

"No need for that. They understand that this world is a sinful one and their mother is now with Jesus."

Jones lowered his voice.

"Strangled, from the appearance of it."

Thornton took a long, shallow breath.

"Anything else?"

"There'll be an autopsy."

"Let me know when you have the report. I want to read it."

"That's your right, Pastor, but from my experience it's better if a family doesn't have all the details of the examination and is satisfied with just the official cause and manner of death."

Thornton's eyes became even darker.

"My wife was murdered. When she died, her soul ascended to heaven. I have no emotional attachment to the body she left behind."

"I understand," Jones said.

"You do? I'm surprised. Sundays you hunt while others are in church."

"I hunt every day."

"Admirable dedication." A small smile, like a crack in hardened clay, creased Thornton's mouth. "I'm also committed, but it's to a cause. With God's help, we will expose the morally corrupt who profit from wickedness and are the servants of Satan. My wife's death won't stop this crusade. Maybe that's what you should understand."

"You think Mrs. Thornton was murdered because of you?"

"To send a message. But the only ones I hear come from God. I have faith that this tragedy will lead not only to the conviction of one heinous criminal but the elimination of the breeding places of crime—the bordellos and saloons, the social cancer rotting our city."

"I'd like to ask you a few questions."

"Go on."

"After the funeral, when you've had more time to deal with all this."

"I'll be in your office today at two."

"OK, then." Jones got up.

"Sheriff," Rose's father crossed the crimson Persian rug, steadied himself by putting his hand on a marble table. "My daughter wore a wristwatch with the initials R.P. engraved on the back. Prindle's my last name. Rose was so happy when I gave it to her. She had just turned 16. I want to make sure she's buried wearing it."

"It wasn't on her wrist, and we didn't find anything when searching the yard for evidence. I'll have the funeral home double check her clothing. I'm sorry."

"Thank you," Prindle answered, his voice lifeless. He returned to his place of shadows by the children.

Jones paused at the parlor door.

"Pastor, did Mrs. Thornton have any money when she left the house?"

"The four dollars I gave her for groceries and the picture show."

"Thank you. Again, my condolences."

On his way out a young woman carrying a meat pie bumped against him.

"Sorry," she said, shyly looking away. She put her dish with the other food, Jones seeing that only hers had a name on it. Hazel.

Outside, he cranked the engine of his runabout, and drove to the Perkins mansion.

Fog obscuring the building floated in ghostly waves over the black rocks jutting from the hill. Strong and used to the steep climb, he quickly reached the large bronze front door taken from a basilica in Italy and depicting the vision of Peter, the words, Rise Peter Kill and Eat, embossed in the metal.

The door opened and Jones looked up at Bor, a hulking, broad shouldered man wearing a black cut-away, the long scar across his neck deep and thick. He led down a hallway of mosaic tiles and marble, the passage's candles dim in the fog-like dust, the dusty outline of frames and loose, dangling wires all that remained of the paintings that once hung on these walls painted with a motif of twisted and thorny vines.

At the end of the cavernous foyer, an unused fireplace added its coldness to the room's emptiness, the only furnishings a couch at one end and a chair at the other, both covered by sheets. The grand staircase rose toward a chandelier hanging from the leaking vaulted ceiling, water seeping into the fixture's incandescent bulbs.

On the balconied second floor, Jones passed tall red and purple stained-glass windows black in the murky light, turned at the marble statue of a headless woman, and followed Bor along the row of leaden windows ending at the office of Roscoe Perkins.

"Shut it, Jones!" Perkins pointed a finger at the door. "It's goddamn freezing!"

Bor stoked the coals.

"I could be in Miami. They read newspapers; they have whores."

Perkins wore a plantation hat, white suit, and red vest. When anger wasn't turning his face pink with crimson blotches, his white, Van Dyke mustache added the only color to his translucent skin. He cursed and chewed tobacco, would never dip snuff, and gave the appearance of a Southern gentleman born and raised in New York City's Hell's Kitchen. Perkins shivered and complained about the cold, but the darkness in his eyes made them look as if they were made of black ice.

"A murder, Jones, a fucking murder right under your fucking nose! Two blocks from the station! Where were you?"

"At home, sir."

"At home sleeping with Dorcas while a woman was strangled and raped!"

"I'm waiting for the report."

"That's right, let's not be hasty. Maybe the murderer ripped her clothes off because he wanted to tickle her."

"He only tore her bloomers."

"Who gives a fuck! She's dead and we've got a problem!" Perkins spat tobacco juice at a porcelain spittoon, hitting the opening three feet away. "I've got interests, Jones, lucrative ones, and you're paid to make sure they stay that way. The story's out. Half the town saw her before you got your ass over there. The *Gazette* will report on the progress of the investigation and the arrest of the murderer. I'm sure he'll be someone with no connection to the South End.

"We keep a lid on this for a week—I'm not worried about Henderson and his college boy. People read the *Blade* for the obituaries and articles about bird watching and growing prize-winning zucchinis." Perkins cackled. "*One week*. Find the bastard and all this dies down. What have you done so far?"

"Taken the first steps."

"Perfect, Sheriff! Just like a baby! I want answers! Do you hear me?" Perkins hit his small, veined hand on the wheelchair's armrest.

"Pastor Thornton thinks his wife was murdered because of his work with the Civic Council."

"That's dangerous. It gives the gnat a larger voice. Maybe the good people of Stone Valley, half of them customers of our saloons and brothels, will begin listening to him and his collection of simps."

"Mrs. Thornton wore a watch and Saturday night, according to her husband, had money in her purse. The watch is missing, the money's gone. Maybe she spent it but we haven't found anything she bought. I noticed the indentation on her finger. The wedding ring had been taken off."

"Excellent! Robbery and lust! That's the story! I'll expect an arrest by Sunday. It'll be an answer to everyone's prayers."

"I'll do my best," Jones said.

"Sure you will, but most likely that won't be enough. If you don't meet the deadline, Bor will help. He'll get you a Negro, maybe one coming here looking to take a quarry job from one of our Bolshevik Italians. I'd prefer a black murderer. A white man requires a trial. That's bad publicity. A Negro is easier to hang. Just rile up the mob, black man rapes white woman. Perfect! It works in the South, why not here? We're all the same. Remember this, Sheriff. Because he can't speak, there's a beautiful simplicity to Bor. He just acts, and never with any ambiguity."

Perkins turned off the gas lamp near him, mansion darkness smothering the coal's smoldering light.

"Isn't this better? Everything hidden! But Hell's warm, thank God for that! Bor! More fire!"

Whenever he left the mansion, Jones hunted small animals for their fur. Today he thought about tracking a moose. They were difficult to find. Solitary, lumbering, they lived deep in the woods and had keen senses. The only one he'd ever killed had been, at first, just a flash of antlers seen through thick vegetation. He'd approached quietly, found the bull munching dandelions by a stream. Not knowing it had been shot, the moose looked around curious about the rifle sound, then dropped over dead.

The Negro Perkins wants is like that. He's a worker, home for lunch, or maybe a returning soldier having a drink and grateful he didn't die in the war. The man is living, unaware death is in him if Roscoe Perkins pulls the trigger.

Am I dead too, not hearing the sound the bribe made when I took my first one from him?

Someone murdered Rose Thornton. Maybe the motive was political, maybe she died during a violent rape. Whatever the reason, I have one week to find the killer or become an accomplice to another murder.

So what if I am.

My parents were right. Stay strong, don't be stupid. I'll keep order without getting in Perkins's way. Why care about someone I never met and who probably doesn't know the difference between a tom and a hen.

But no moose hunting today.

I have a case to solve.

That meant finding the owner of the handkerchief used in the murder.

As the city prospered, the downtown expanded north adding shops, the movie theatre, a bank, diner, Victrola agent, bakery, and Woolworth's on one side of the street, on the other, the Opera House, law and telegraph offices, telephone exchange, hardware, and the brick and granite municipal building with the police station and jail next door. A block over from North Main, between the pharmacy and general store, Murphy & Weaver Billiards and Bowling Alley offered *The Best Place in Town To Spend A Pleasant Hour.* Next to it, the Stone Valley Laundry.

Jones went inside.

"Is this laundry mark yours?" he asked the owner.

"It is," she answered.

"Do you remember the customer's name?"

She told him.

"You're sure?"

"Been doing his clothes for twenty years. You see this needs washing. His fingerprints are probably all over it."

"You can lift them from hard surfaces and soft ones like clay, but not from fabrics."

He thanked her, put the handkerchief in his pocket, and left.

* * *

Built in 1860, thirty years before Stone Valley's boom, the wooden two-story Old Town Hall had once been the central meeting place for farmers trying to find additional ways to sell their milk. By 1890, politicians, quarry owners, and railroad men, all interested in making more money through the transport and sale of granite, met here to plan. The result—prosperity. Immigrants dug and carved stone, sickened from the dust, died, and were replaced. Strikes ended, sometimes violently. Mechanization in the quarries reduced the number of men needed and increased profits. Granite for foundations and monuments continued the demand.

Also, by 1890, what started as one small bar and a tin-roof, two-room bordello, had become the South End. Alcohol and women in its two blocks of ramshackle buildings brought in customers from the prosperous North Side.

As the North and South parts of Stone Valley expanded, Town Hall Street became nothing more than an alley dividing these two sections of town.

The rich still met, but now in Roscoe Perkins's mansion.

The Old Town Hall had one tenant. It's first floor cluttered with broken wagon wheels of various sizes, **Ride THE NARROW Gauge** signs, rail spikes, sledge hammers, and rusted saws used when new to cut blocks of ice, Jones climbed swaying steps and entered the *Blade's* large, musty, printing room, its overhead beams cracked and covered with yellow-brown fungi. Light dimmed by dust drifted down through holes in the roof; clumps of dirt squatted in the spaces between the floorboards.

Next to the drum cylinder printing press in the room's center, a typesetter sat slumped in a chair, the only proof he was asleep and not dead the occasional dust-filled snort interrupting his timeworn breathing too faint to be heard. Purchased from "Buffalo Bill" Cody by Chester Henderson's father and brought to Vermont, the press had fascinated young Chester. His father having decided to hunt treasure rather than publish a newspaper, at 17 Chester started the *Blade,* a twice weekly publication reporting only good news. He later added tips on gardening and a horoscope column. His son, Felix, back from college, thought himself a journalist.

For Jones, that was a problem.

"Afternoon, Chester," Jones said while passing the publisher's office, its shelves crammed with models of planets, moons, telescopes, binoculars, books listing the trajectory of celestial objects, crystals, skunk skulls, and stuffed songbirds.

Hunched over one of the star charts on his cluttered desk, Henderson nodded without looking up.

In the small office next to his, Penelope Wimple slowly, reverently, as if touching sacred scripture, moved the finger of one of her white-gloved hands down a column of words in her *Oxford English Dictionary,* her intent to find the most florid way to describe the muddy-boot life of an old farmer who had just died. Death, for her, meant the chance to write poetry people would read. When she found the right adjective or better yet, several of them she could string together in alliterative purple glory, the enormous white plume on her hat shook from the vibrations shivering through her never wed body from its constricted hobble skirt to her feathery head.

When seeing Jones, Felix Henderson pushed his chair back from his desk and quickly went to greet him.

"Hello, Sheriff. I know you're busy investigating the murder, but I really appreciate you stopping by the *Blade* to tell me what's happening. I'll print a special edition!"

Pale and boney, his thinning blond hair thicker than the yellowy mustache he tried to grow, Felix stepped back while pulling nervously on his tiny bowtie. No longer smiling, he had seen when looking up into the sheriff's massive face that Jones wasn't there to collaborate or have a friendly chat.

"You'll report nothing about this murder unless I approve it. There's already been too much talk. Mr. Perkins has agreed to these press restrictions. Do your civic duty, Felix, follow his lead. You wouldn't want to help a murderer get away, would you?"

"No, Sheriff," Felix answered while shaking his head.

"Good. Help your father publish what the *Blade* does best. I always look forward to reading how the stars affect us. I never knew that planting when Venus is in Pisces will grow bigger tomatoes."

The station's Fiddleback wall phone rang, Mabel putting the call through from the town's central exchange.

"I have Doctor Gillespie on the line," she told Jones when he answered.

"Sheriff?"

"Yes, Doctor."

"Can you hear me?'

"Nice and clear."

"I have the autopsy findings. Are you ready?"

"Go on."

"The contents of her stomach had a pea soup thickness—digested vegetables, but when put through a sieve left a small fatty substance, probably meat. This food was eaten two-four hours before her death which I estimate to be sometime between 11 Saturday night and 12:30 Sunday morning.

"Official cause of death—suffocation. The twisting of the hand-kerchief found at the scene pressed the square knot hard against her throat, strangling her. From the bruises on her hips and thighs, I determined that she kicked up and out in an effort to get away."

"Officer Grange found her lying face down."

"I know. Curious. There was spermatozoa."

"Not surprising."

"The intercourse postmortem."

Jones stopped writing.

"I'll send you my written report."

"Mabel." The sheriff knew she was listening. "This is confidential police business. I'm sure you not only like your job but want to go home to your family every night."

He hung up the receiver.

A dark, stiffly gliding presence, Pastor Thornton arrived in Jones's office promptly at two, walked to the chair in front of the desk and sat with his long legs crossed. Jones hurried over. Dropping down heavily onto his desk chair, he faced the pastor.

"Thank you for coming in. This shouldn't take long."

"That's good to know." Thornton picked a piece of lint from his trousers.

"When did you last see your wife?"

"Right after supper. She left for the pictures."

"Do you remember what time you ate?"

"Five-thirty. I like my dinner served on schedule. Our daily meal at the table provides another opportunity for me to teach my children."

"Did Mr. Prindle eat with you."

"As always. He listens, finds what I say valuable. So did Rose."

"He can verify the time."

"If verification is needed."

"Mrs. Thornton had four dollars for groceries and the movie."

"Yes, and I expected change."

"The one playing—"

"*Mr. Logan.* I don't attend the picture shows, unfortunately my wife enjoyed them. The actors are on morphine and the subject matter promotes adultery, atheism, homosexuality, and vice. But this one does interest me. One of the characters is a corrupt sheriff."

"Evening showings are 6:45 and 8:30. Do you know which one Mrs. Thornton went to?"

"No. I wasn't interested. Every Saturday night she went alone."

"To the same picture?"

"She was a good wife and mother. That made up for her lack of curiosity and rather flat intellect. She was also an excellent cook."

"The coroner determined that the murder happened Saturday night or Sunday morning between the hours of 11:00 and 12:30. He also told me that Mrs. Thornton had eaten two to four hours before she died. If we take the earliest possibility, four hours and time of death, 11, your wife had a second meal at 7:00 and wasn't at the 6:45 movie."

"Then why did you ask me?"

"Maybe she ate later. Was that with someone?"

"I wouldn't know. I'll review the written report and make my own conclusions."

"You were at a Civic Council meeting."

"Until 10. I can provide you with our minutes and the names of those there."

"Afterwards?"

"I went out with our board of directors. They are common men, that's true, but hard-working ones with families and the passion to purge Stone Valley of sin by swinging the sword of Christ down on its disease-ridden dens of iniquity. You know them well, don't you sheriff?"

"Your board members?"

"The whorehouses and saloons that pay you and your employer, Roscoe Perkins."

"I am a city employee, Pastor Thornton, enforcing the law."

"You prostrate yourself before pharaoh."

"How long were you with the others?"

"Until I went home."

"When was that?"

"Around 1 am.

"Late for someone who had to preach in the morning."

"You mean, give a sermon. I am never tired when speaking the Word of God."

"What did you do all night?"

"We went to a dance at the Socialist Hall, then to Tim Calhoun's house where his wife made us egg sandwiches. Back at the dance we listened to the music, gathered at Peter Colby's home and talked about what men find important when united in a common cause. We ate more sandwiches. I drank one glass of wine. If that makes me a hypocrite, then I am one. But Jesus himself turned water into wine and at the Last Supper, spoke of it as his blood.

"Tim, Peter, Vince Gallard and Rory Owens, they were with me all night. You can ask them if at any time I left to strangle my wife."

"Did you enjoy the Negro jazz band?"

"Very much. It was Dixieland and, Sheriff Jones, all the musicians were white. Are we done?"

"Almost. When did you notice your wife wasn't home?"

"When I got there. She was usually back before me, but I wasn't worried. Saturday nights she'd leave our children with her father and forgetting about her other household duties, go to the pictures. Did I like it? No, but I wasn't her master. Rose was quite childlike. She liked reading about fashion and astrology. I spoke to her regarding the sin of vanity and how the occult exposes us to spirits other than God's. She didn't listen and after the shows I'm sure looked in store windows and star gazed. But around four in the morning the Holy Spirit awakened me. True enough, Rose wasn't in her bed. Mr. Prindle and I looked for her, then we went home thinking she might be back. I prayed and was ready to report her missing, when church members brought me the news."

"You waited for me in your parlor."

"I'm waiting for you to do your job. Find my wife's murderer."

After the pastor left, Jones drove home. Dorcas served him a beer and chaser, glanced at herself in the mirror behind the bar, then sat down next to a customer.

4

Tuesday Day Two

VERMONT PASTOR'S WIFE STRANGLED
NAKED BODY LEFT IN GARDEN

"Today's edition of the *Phoenix,* Sheriff. Brought it straight from Boston. Thought you'd like your own copy." The reporter stepped closer to the desk. "How's the case going? Any leads? Suspects? What about motive? A love affair gone wrong? Was she violated?"

"No comment."

"Sure, I get it. I'm checking around myself. This is a big story. Keep me informed and I'll make sure you get credit as the man who cracked the case wide open. All New England, hell, the whole United States, will know you're a hero. Of course, that requires giving me exclusive access."

"And if I don't?"

"I won't need you."

"Stay away from Pastor Thornton. He's a man who just lost his wife."

"You're the boss. Name's Shapiro. I'm staying at the Arc should you need to find me."

"Thanks for this." Jones slowly ripped the front page in two, shoved the pieces and the rest of the newspaper into the wastebasket.

"Too bad. I was going to autograph that. Nice meeting you, Sheriff. I'll stay in touch." Shapiro left whistling.

Jones knew before answering who was calling.

"I've seen it! Fucking reporter's handing out copies like they're candy! Lid's off, nice work, Sheriff! Now I'll have every reporter in the world snooping around here. Who spilled their guts? Was it Henderson's son, that Willie boy? I heard he was in the telegraph office. Find out what he sent. Bor will teach the bastard a lesson."

"Lots of people saw the body, Mr. Perkins. I met with Felix. It wasn't him."

"That telegraph and the murderer. I'm not paying you to sit on your ass!"

Perkins hung up.

A sunny day for Stone Valley, the sun visible in its lonely place above the mountains but smudged by the fog looked as if the sky had a cataractous eye. Jones passed the municipal building and Mabel's telephone exchange, a little bell ringing as he opened the telegraph's office door.

Wearing a green visor and headphones, the operator leaned forward toward his large desk, the electric printing telegraph on top, wet cell batteries underneath, and using the telegraph key, finished transmitting. He turned, and standing up felt the headphones yanked off, their connecting wire not long enough to keep them on his head.

"I'm wondering, Noah, if you have a copy of Felix Henderson's telegram. I'm not mistaken, am I? He did send one yesterday?"

"Yes…"

"And the copy?"

"I transmit from the original."

"Which, of course, you kept. Let me have it."

The operator wiped his large round glasses that each year got a little thicker, took the telegram from his desk drawer.

"This went to the Boston *Phoenix*. Anywhere else?"

"AP member newspapers."

"AP? What's that?"

"Associated Press. They all have teletypewriters in their newsrooms."

"Hmm. OK. Let me know what else goes out about the murder. This isn't a request, it's a police order. Have a seat."

Jones pulled the headphones down over the operator's ears.

While returning to the station, he saw the increased traffic on North Main Street, the normal five to six black cars now twenty as newspaper reporters drove into town. He waited for Grange to get back from his morning beat.

"Handcuff Felix Henderson and bring him in."

Jones shut his office door, walked over and stared into the eyes of the moose head mounted on the wall.

You knew I was there but didn't look at me. I know why. My eyes are what yours are now, clay and glass, nothing in them for anyone to see.

He took a bottle of rum from the moose's mouth.

* * *

"He's in a cell," Grange reported. "Came along without a fuss, except for the crying. Wanna talk to him?"

"Not now. Pratt all set?"

"Locked in at Mother Mae's but with a good bed, magazines, jam, biscuits, cheese and crackers. She's planning on bringing him bread stew. He ain't complaining. Hell, I wouldn't mind being locked up there myself."

"We'll take your car, less obvious. That's the plan, Grange, keep away from anyone asking questions. You're not to say anything, understand?"

"That's easy, I'm not the gassy type."

They drove up Winter Road, passing the Colton garden. In their rush to look around the yard, reporters and photographers had pushed past the two deputies trying to secure the crime scene, knocked over part of the fence, and with heavy feet trampled the ice into muddy ground.

"I wanted it left white and frozen," Jones remarked.

"To preserve the evidence."

"Out of respect for death."

"Should we go back and do something?"

"Yeah, shoot them all."

A reporter kept knocking on the front door of the Colton home while others tapped on its windows covered by thick dark curtains.

At Summer and Pearl, Jones asked Grange to stop in front of the hotel.

"That's his room. He had a clear view of it."

"Could definitely see the body," the deputy agreed.

"OK, let's go."

Outside, standing by her door, Mother Mae waited for them. A heavyset, older woman dressed in black, a lace collar and silver cross around her neck, a tatting of lace covering her head, her brown eyes not unkind, her mouth curling only slightly downward, she didn't allow men inside her boarding house. Strict, but not inflexible, she made exceptions. When Sheriff Jones wanted Pratt detained, and in secret, she agreed to put him in one of her rooms. She had worked with Rose at the Red Cross during the war and would do whatever she could to help find the young woman's killer.

Mother Mae wasn't worried that Pratt could be dangerous. She owned a shotgun, carried a revolver and Bowie Knife, and having killed the man who tried to attack her, knew it would be even easier to shoot or stab a boy.

She opened the door for the policemen, gave Jones the key to Pratt's room.

His head propped up on a pillow, cracker crumbs on his shirt, Pratt put his comic book down and grinned.

"Hi there, fellas.

"Officer Grange."

"Right. Sorry." Pratt yawned and hands behind his head, leaned back.

"And this is Sheriff Jones."

"Uh huh."

Jones grabbed Pratt's legs, yanked him to the floor, then kicked him in the ribs with the steel toe of his boot.

"Sit your ass in that chair."

He hobbled over, holding his side. His long black hair and curly beard masked most of the soft, rosy-tinged skin of his face but not his eyes. Pain, alertness, and fear making them childlike in size, he looked like a small boy waiting not for a beating but something worse, the unknown.

"I ask the questions, you answer."

Pratt nodded.

"I want to hear it."

"Yes sir."

"Yes, Sheriff Jones. Thank you, Officer Grange."

Pratt repeated it.

"I'm keeping you here because you told Officer Grange about a body before anyone, except the killer, even knew Mrs. Thornton had been murdered. Plus, I don't like the way you look. When did you arrive in Stone Valley?"

"Friday. I came by bus from Northfield hoping to find work in a quarry."

"You lived in Northfield?"

"And lots of other places. I was born in Rutland but left home at 15. Both of my parents are drunks."

"Any run-ins with the law?"

"No sir."

"How did you support yourself?"

"Farmhand, carried bricks, swept up in a cotton mill, did some lumbering."

"Tie this for me. Use a square knot. It's simple."

"Will you show me how?"

Jones took the rope back.

"Tell me about Saturday. How did you spend the day?"

"Didn't do much at first. I had breakfast, walked around downtown, looked at some cars for sale, bought a hotdog and Tastykake, then listened to jazz at the Victrola store. When I left an old woman came over and told me she gives supper parties and asked if I'd like to go to one that night and meet a girl who, even though I looked like a wolf, would be interested in me. It'd cost a dollar to get in, four for supper and a room, drinks extra, and my date might want something."

"This woman introduce herself?"

"Mrs. Porter."

"Did you go?"

"Yessir. That's when I first saw her."

"Who?"

"The dead woman."

"I don't understand."

"I got to the party and there were a lot of women, but one was different than the others, really pretty but more natural looking, not painted up at all. She seemed shy, stood watching people, but wasn't trying to get noticed. I smiled at her and she came over. We talked for a few minutes."

"About what."

"Me. She was real nice."

"You're saying the woman you met at Mrs. Porter's Saturday night was the woman you later found dead? Be very careful how you answer, Pratt."

"The same person. I'm sure of it. I remember the face and there was a mole near her eye."

"Did she tell you her name?"

"No, and I didn't ask."

"What else did she do besides somehow find you interesting?"

"Drink and dance with her date."

"What did he look like?"

"He wore a nice suit, had sideburns and a waxed mustache, probably thought himself a dandy. But in my books, he wasn't anything special."

"But you noticed this pretty lady right away and when she left you followed her."

"No, I stayed at Mrs. Porter's the whole night."

"I want details."

"Mrs. Porter had a strict schedule. At 6:30 there was supper, 7:15 she wanted everyone drinking and having fun. My date was a real keen girl, a redhead, but quiet. Hattie Donato or maybe D'Angela, something Italian. She told me her mother was Irish and her father, a stone carver from Italy, had just died. After a few drinks she was laughing and joking. We danced, got blotto, then went to our room. I left at 11:30, don't know when Hattie did. Mrs. Porter has clocks all over the place—on walls and mantels, tables and near beds, some ringing, some chiming. We all knew that we had to leave before 12 or pay extra. I heard that at midnight she takes a loaded shotgun with her while checking every room."

"You walked back to the hotel?"

"Yes."

"Up Winter Street? Across Summer to Pearl?"

"Sounds right. I had a map. Like I said, I'd only been in town a couple of days."

"What time did you reach the Arc?"

"After 12. The night clerk wasn't there, I saw he hadn't even punched in. This was his shift, and I needed my key. I planned on giving him an earful, but he told me he'd been using the water closet, so we had a couple drinks and that was that."

"How much after 12? Five minutes? Ten? Thirty?"

"Five, yeah, that's it."

"Grange, in your estimation, how long would it take a young man walking at a normal pace, not like yours of course, to reach the Colton garden from Mrs. Porter's home?"

"It's nine blocks all together, I'd say 18 minutes."

"Then to the Arc?"

"Another two blocks, four minutes."

"I've always been good at numbers, Pratt. Never needed pencil or paper to do them. From what Deputy Grange just told us, you should have been at the hotel at 11:52 not 12:05. There's a missing 13 minutes."

"I probably got the times wrong, that's all."

"But you seemed so sure of them just now."

"I don't want to be disrespectful, Sheriff. May I ask you something?"

"Go ahead."

"Why does it matter how long it took me?"

"That, Pratt, is an excellent question! Mrs. Rose Thornton, the friend you made at Porter's little party, was between 11 Saturday night and 12:30 Sunday morning, murdered, raped, robbed, and left in an icy backyard. You were in the area at that time. Although I've never killed a woman or needed to rape or rob one, I'm convinced that in those unaccounted for 13 minutes you could have committed all three crimes *and* celebrated by having a drink while sitting next to her naked corpse."

"*I didn't strangle her or do anything else!*" Pratt shouted, leaning forward as if ready to propel himself from the chair.

"Did I say strangle?"

"I—I saw the handkerchief."

"I know you did. Do you have a car?"

"No! Didn't you hear me? I took the bus."

Jones slapped the boy's face.

"Tone, Mr. Pratt, tone. Can you drive one?"

"Ye-yes."

"I might never have known about your connection to Mrs. Thornton. So why did we meet? Why am I talking to you now? Because you decided to lead Officer Grange to a body. Does this prove innocence or that you returned to admire your handywork? There's another, better explanation. Wouldn't it be suspicious if you didn't tell anyone about the dead woman you could clearly see from your window at the Arc?"

"I didn't do it," Pratt said, looking down, his voice trembling.

"Cheer up. I saw Mother Mae has this month's copy of *Ladies Home Journal*. I'll make sure she brings it up with your stew."

"Think he killed her?" Grange asked as they walked to the car.

"There's no evidence of Rose being forced into the garden, no drag marks across the ice, so I'm guessing she knew the man who strangled her. Pratt admitted they met. He placed himself at the murder scene. Do I think he's the murderer? I'm working on it.

"We have those tire tracks on Winter. Maybe she was driven to the Colton's yard. You won't be back on your beat for a while. Check at the hotel and see if Pratt has a car parked there, then find out at the bus station if they know anything about him. If he told us the truth, that he doesn't own a motorcar, maybe he borrowed or stole one."

"Rose Thornton, a sporting woman…" The deputy shook his head.

"People will judge her because of it but she was more than that."

"Maybe the pastor won't find out."

"You saw the reporters, Grange. I can't arrest them all. Perkins isn't going to like this. If Rose was at Porter's place, that's a South End connection. While you're out, see what you can learn about Pratt's time in Northfield and Rutland. Also, take a man and search his room at the Arc. Do you still go on your nightly rides?"

"Sometimes."

"Have spells?"

"Not in a while."

"We'll get our murderer, you can bet on that. You drive."

Except for the sound of Jones's cracking knuckles, they rode in silence.

* * *

"How are you doing, Felix?"

Henderson gripped the cell door.

"Why am I in here? What have I done?"

"Lied to me."

"No, never —"

"You went to college, probably studied why people do things. I'm not educated but I have my theories too. Liars keep lying hoping that after a while no one will remember the truth. It's like covering yourself in horseshit thinking those around you will get used to the smell. You stink, Felix. I have the telegram. You sent the story out."

"I only said what the whole town knows. I want to help you find the killer."

Jones grabbed him by the bowtie and pulled his face to the bars.

"I can't legally keep you in here or stop you from digging into other people's lives. I'm the sheriff, I have to follow the law. But Roscoe Perkins has his own way of handling things. It's effective and comes with a name. Bor.

Sweat streaked Felix's forehead, seeped through the scattered hairs of his mustache.

"I told Perkins you weren't the one who brought the reporters to town. He wants the telegram. I have it. One word from me and his cretin visits the *Blade* to see you *and* your dad. Why did you do it?"

"I want to become a reporter for the AP, have the *Blade* accepted as a member newspaper."

"Astrology and squash alongside the *Phoenix* and *Times* reports on Italian delegates to the International Peace Conference. Yes, I can see that. Amazing that a college boy can be such a dumb ass. Last chance, Felix."

He unlocked the cell.

* * *

The South End. Quiet during the day, no fistfights or muggings, the drunks having staggered home, the North End men, again dressed in somber suits and back at work, forgotten by the prostitutes they'd met.

In brothels decorated with fringed lampshades and frayed, horsehair chairs, the faded embossed wallpaper colored by stains, women preened in front of broken gilded mirrors, their faces in cracked glass tinted by the pale, green-white light from gas chandeliers.

From weathered buildings, prostitutes wearing nightgowns spotless and white, their long black hair combed high, stood on balconies or sat in windows, and while practicing their smiles looked with faraway eyes toward the mountains.

Silent in the afternoon's fog and mist, the incorporeal voices from South End nights haunted the air while waiting for darkness and rum to once again let them speak, the sounds of seduction and loneliness always the same.

Although the most dilapidated South End brothel and bar, *Queens End,* had a bright red door and proudly displayed a large sign mocking the Murphy and Weaver billiard/bowling alley one.

The Very Best Place in Stone Valley To Spend
A Pleasant Hour With Balls and a Stick

Even the South End had its poorer section, the wooden sidewalk in front of the saloons and brothels ending in the mud of Shanty Town. First generation immigrants, recently arrived Negroes, and the unemployed, lived here in shacks or if they had the means, in a boarding house where lodgers never saw live rats, the landlady's large, well-fed cats leaving only a head or tail behind in the rooms.

Of all the buildings in the South End, Mrs. Porter's home was the largest, best kept, and only two blocks from the North End's Old Town Hall. The front gate of her iron fence opened onto a brick walkway lined on both sides by the bare branches of rose bushes that in spring bloomed crimson and white. Flower beds had been covered with straw and chicken manure. In a fountain a stone boy peed frozen water. At the front door of this Victorian house, two winged cupids and a bust of Venus greeted visitors. In back, strings of hanging lanterns swung in the wind over love couches stacked for winter.

Her windows were stained glass, the wood shellacked and dark. Every room had a clock and except the parlor, a bed, the cot in the kitchen next to the coal burning range the least expensive accommodation to rent for a few hours.

It was a house of trysts and clocks where lust, or love, ended at midnight.

Jones parked in back, noticed tire marks in the muddy yard as he walked to the front door.

"Sheriff. My, how unexpected."

Spindly, with a long neck and large crest of white hair resembling the feathers on a Polish chicken, Nellie Porter nervously jerked her head, her eye movement darting but purposeful. She could quickly scan North Street for prey or, like now, see danger.

Jones knew her well. As he did with all the saloon owners and madams in the South End, every Sunday he collected from her Pickens's share of her weekly take. But Porter's business model was different. She too made money by selling alcohol but her main source of income was renting rooms to the men and women she brought together for a night.

Porter had developed a skill for finding lonely or bored housewives or those who simply wanted a good time. To entice one, she'd say she'd been contacted by an interested gentleman to act as his intermediary. Getting a man to fill the role was easy, sex a foolproof motivator.

By charging four dollars per bedroom, per night, she doubled what a standard rental would have brought in. In addition to the liquor sales, she also had a one-dollar introduction fee.

Pickens's cut was a known business expense, the sheriff's presence on a Tuesday a disquieting change of routine. Head bobbing even more, her eyes shifted in new directions.

"I'm investigating the murder of Rose Thornton. Your name was mentioned." Jones walked past her and, in the parlor, sat on a new, upholstered chair. When Porter quickly joined him, he moved the chair in front of hers and held her eyes steady by looking straight at them.

"Sheriff Jones—"

"Before you say anything, know that whatever you tell me now I'll have you repeat under oath. Perjure yourself and you'll end up in state prison. Was Mrs. Thornton here Saturday night?"

"Yes, I let her in."

"What time was that?"

"6:30. That's when our supper parties start."

"You arranged a date for her?"

"With a nice man, clean and well-dressed.

"Name."

"George Higgins. She'd been with him before."

"How often?"

"I'll check my notes, but I'd say four times in one month. That was unusual for her. She liked different men. Rose was a good-looking woman. Very popular. Getting dates for her was duck soup." Mrs. Porter smiled, her small teeth pointed and sharp.

"Mrs. Thornton, the pastor's wife, was a regular customer?"

"The men are my customers, Sheriff. They are the ones who pay."

"She had been coming to your parties—for what? Months?"

"Years. She started before her first child was born, took time off, then started up again. Every Saturday night."

"Do you know where this Higgins lives?"

"Everyone has to register."

"I want his address. What food did you serve on Saturday?"

"Same as always. Deviled eggs, corn and beans, rice pudding."

"No meat?"

"I'm a good businesswoman, Sheriff. No sense wasting money."

"When did you last see Mrs. Thornton?"

"Around nine. She was in the parlor, laughing and talking to all the men, George Higgins just one of them. Rose always looked bashful at first but warmed up and could razzle-dazzle anyone. After introductions are made and payment given, I leave the couples alone so they can get better acquainted. I check the rooms at midnight. If a man is still there, he pays another four dollars, no supper or date included. Rose was gone, the women never stay."

"There's tire tracks out back."

"Montgomery Braxton dropped a car off on Saturday so my customer, a young gentleman interested in buying it, could take the machine for a spin. I told Mr. Braxton that the first thing a man does when arriving is pay me."

"Did this one drive the car while he was here?"

"I left him the key."

"Check your book, I want his name."

"I already know it. Butch Pratt. He's easy to remember. I took a chance with him, and it worked out. I found a girl who likes the hairy type. He has a room at the Arc."

Jones got up.

"If anyone comes around asking questions don't answer them or I'll be back with the paddy wagon."

When driving away, he saw the *Phoenix* reporter knock on Mrs. Porter's front door.

Shapiro walks with a limp. He'd be easy to kill.

At the *Queen's End* Dorcas brought him a beer then continued mopping the floor. When she finished, they went up to her room.

The lovemaking always quick, what they liked best was afterward when they faced each other and talked.

"What's wrong?" She gently put her small, calloused hand on the side of his large head, her brown hair, dull and thinning, falling across a dry ashen face caused by using too much powder for too many years.

"I have five days to find a murderer."

"What happens if you don't?"

"A Negro dies."

"I don't understand."

Jones sat up, Dorcas's hand dropping to the sheet. She leaned back against the headboard.

"Before the murder, did anyone, except Thornton and his Civic Council boy scouts, try to do anything about the South End? We know this place, it's where we both make money and understand how important it is for even God-fearing, hymn singing men, proud of their wives and children, to have a little fun from time to time if done in secret and not near church or home. Perkins wants the reporters gone so the story about Rose ends without causing any damage to his businesses. I'm the corrupt sheriff who will make sure he continues getting money from boozers and prostitutes. All it requires is an arrest. If not the real murderer, any black man will do."

"You've decided on that."

"It's not a choice."

"Actions always are."

"No, Dorcas, you're wrong. If I don't kill a bear, it's not because I was born merciful but at that moment a different thought took over, maybe because of what I once heard from Pastor Thornton in a sermon." He smirked. "We're all controlled by something or someone. For me, it's Roscoe Perkins."

"What will you lose?"

"What I am. And you."

"I don't need the *Queen's End*. Even when prohibition closes all the bars, I'll still have work."

"Tell people they can't drink and they'll want to even more. Perkins will get richer."

"We could both leave. We planned that once."

"She'd be 20 this May."

Jones got dressed, carefully pinned his badge on.

"I have a few leads. Rose had a date Saturday night and I know the owner of the handkerchief used to strangle her. There's a young grifter I've got locked up at Mae's. And there's Grange."

"That sweet man?"

"Sweet and strange. He takes prostitutes for rides."

"That doesn't mean he kills them."

"I learned that even before she had children, Rose was one of Porter's dating women. Why? Money? The thrill."

"Find out, Sheriff, and maybe that will help you solve the case."

After he left, Dorcas took little booties from a scratched end table and lying back on the bed positioned one on each breast.

Jones parked in front of the station. In his office he found a note.

Sheriff Jones

> *Saturday Night I was with pals of mine.*
> *We came into town drunk and left even drunker.*
> *There was a woman standing outside the movie house.*
> *I got out of the wagon, ran over and danced a little*
> *with her. She was scared. I'm married, have children,*
> *I shouldn't have done what I did and I'm sorry.*
> *I've been reading about the woman who was killed.*
> *Maybe she's the one. It must have been just a*
> *few minutes after eleven when I saw her. I know*
> *how long it took for us to get into town. Can't*
> *tell you where we came from. I don't want to get*
> *pulled into this thing.*
> *Hope you find the killer.*

"Anyone know where this came from?"

"A boy brought it in," one of the officers in the outer office answered. "Told me a man on a horse gave him a nickel to deliver it, then rode off."

"Let's question the kid."

"Might take awhile to find, I never saw him before."

Jones took a deep breath.

"Perfect."

"Sorry, Sheriff?"

"Nothing. I'm going for a walk."

Jones wondered if he'd just gotten a message from the murderer. He could go to the South End, ask questions about a wagon full of Saturday night drunks, maybe get a lead, but more likely, by chasing a ghost, waste the few days he had left.

But the letter did have one important fact.

On Saturday night, a little after 11 pm, someone saw Rose Thornton at the Bijou.

On North Main Street, Jones walked to the corner, smiled at a baby in the stroller next to him, then thought about stepping in front of the oncoming trolley.

5

Wednesday Day Three

WAS ROSE MURDERED
AT THE PORTER HOME?

Although Jones felt Lance Shapiro creeping up behind him, he knew, for now, the reporter was still a few steps behind. Shapiro hadn't pried much information from Mrs. Porter but had learned that Rose was at the party house Saturday night. What he'd filed under his *Phoenix* headline had few details and many questions.

Could she have been killed there, strangled while the other guests were in their rooms and Nellie Porter asleep? How would the murderer have moved the body to that ice covered backyard? Wagon? Car or truck? Death has forever sealed this poor woman's lips. Will the facts of the murder remain a mystery or by shinning a light on Mrs. Thornton's past will we learn who committed this horrible crime? I cast no aspersions. The Pastor's Wife was a mother and church going Christian. But we do know this. The coroner has spoken. Between 11:00 Saturday night and 12:30 Sunday morning the life of our Rose of Vermont ended and her soul was taken to be weighed on the scales of Justice by the One who will judge us all.

Jones carefully folded the *Phoenix*. He liked this story and would keep it. Shapiro had missed an important fact. There were no drag or wheel marks in the Colton yard. Rose might have been driven there but she went in alive. When tracking deer, only an experienced hunter could tell the difference between the hoof prints of a doe and stag. He hoped Shapiro continued chasing his theory through the woods, increasing the distance between them by looking for scrapes and rubs, while he hunted down a rabid dog.

"Good morning, Felix."

"Uh, hello Sheriff."

Jones heard nervousness at the end of the line.

"I think the reporter for the *Phoenix* is on to something. Don't bother Mrs. Porter but introduce Shapiro to Pitts at Able Truck Hauling then take him to a few of the wagon companies in town. The *Blade* should follow Shapiro's lead. It's shocking, but maybe Rose Thornton was murdered at the Porter house or somewhere else, like the Arc Hotel. That's close to the Colton property. It wouldn't take more than a wheelbarrow to move her body from the hotel to the garden."

"Thank you, Sheriff, all I ever wanted to do was help."

"You'll be helping me and yourself. Shapiro is an important man. Working with him, a Boston reporter, can open doors for you."

"I was thinking about that."

Jones hung up. He knew Shapiro would eventually find the right trail.

Maybe I've bought myself a day.

* * *

Roscoe smelled the carnation in the buttonhole of his tailored suit.

"Do you play chess?"

"No."

"Of course not. Chess requires planning five moves ahead. What we're doing now is checkers. The woman was at Porter's. A Jew reporter connected her to one of my businesses. That business must be cut off as you would a rotted leg to save the body." He hit his stump, his lips curling in cold, malicious merriment. "I knew a woman. Maybe you remember her. Nora. Thought she was an artist. Pretty. Pleasurable. But she betrayed me and became disposable trash. I wonder if that made your Deputy Grange sad. Take you, Sheriff. You've been useful but if in the end you prove as dumb as a bag of hammers and Rose Thornton doesn't stay buried, I'll find a replacement and Bor will help you leave Stone Valley.

"But why worry about that! Just do as I say, and we'll both be happy. Arrest Porter as an accomplice to murder, board up her house, tell the press you're closing in on the murderer and will have him in custody by Sunday.

"Do you know why I'm so cold?"

"You were born that way?" Jones answered.

"That's right, others have too much blood while I have so little. I'm oppressed by the unfairness in life. You and Bor have legs, I'm the one who can't walk!"

Bor poked the coals, shards of light from the sparking flames reddening Perkins's eyes. He reached out as if wanting to bathe himself in the fire.

Where the stained glass on the second floor turned daylight through the window into red and purple night, Jones looked over the railing of the grand staircase. Never joyful or sad, purposely violent and resigned to life, since Sunday he had felt the returning darkness, the sweet call of oblivion. Enveloping the hanging chandelier with its icy frayed wires, the wide black emptiness falling to the foyer's marble floor offered so much more than death by trolley. He could jump and for a few seconds, fly.

He remembered when one Halloween he asked his mother for a ghost costume. She cut an old sheet and draped it over him. There were no holes for eyes. He couldn't see.

"You want to be dead. This is what it's like."

Fog wrapping the town, turning even mountains into white vapor. No stars, no sun. I move inside a fog covered world and only think I see.

She'd hit him, but especially hard when he sat looking at the ground instead of trimming hooves or doing his other chores. He again tasted the blood.

Pull yourself up Jones. Go on. Mother was always right. Don't be an ass.

Down the hill and beyond its black, jagged rocks, he continued feeling the pain caused by Perkins and his mansion, even their shadows, like acidic secretions, made his stomach burn. But he again didn't have time for purification. Instead of hunting and gutting rabbits, he drove to the small home of George Higgins, paint peeling from the clapboard, shafts of thorny weeds poking up through the snow.

A woman opened the door.

"Mrs. Higgins?"

She nodded slightly.

Jones remembered her. She had bumped against him at Pastor Thornton's, her name, Hazel, on her dish. Her long, curly blonde hair pulled back into a bun, she had grey-blue eyes and a fashionable porcelain doll face—pale skin, flushed cheeks, small well-formed lips—none of her appearance caused by cosmetics. Jones knew what painted women looked like.

"I'd like to speak to your husband."

"I'm sorry, he's still at work."

"When will he be home?"

"Hard to say. The superintendent has him in the hole keeping one of the drills oiled."

"Was Mr. Higgins at the quarry yesterday?"

"Yes sir."

"Maybe he has some information about the accident. Tell him I was here, and I'd appreciate it if he dropped by the station tomorrow morning. You knew Mrs. Thornton?"

"We talked in church, sewed for the soldiers, but I wouldn't say we were friends. She was a nice woman and what happened to her so horrible. My only comfort is knowing that when you find the killer and he receives punishment on earth, hell will make his suffering eternal."

"Thank you, Mrs. Higgins. Tomorrow then, at ten."

"I'll let him know." She closed the door.

Ahead of him on the narrow, one lane road, the fog capped logging sleigh slid smoothly over ice. Jones could have passed it but instead of hurrying to question the motorcar dealer, Montgomery Braxton, he slowed down and thought about the three men who had died and why most newspaper readers would never know what happened to them. Only the *Blade* reported the accident, squeezing the story on a back page between an ad for satin skin cream and tooth soap.

Yesterday, part of a wedge-shaped shelf jutting out from the quarry wall had broken off, falling on the driller below, slicing him in two, the fragments then hitting and killing two men on a lower section, one chaining a large block for lifting by a crane, the other cleaning up smaller pieces of grout. Elmer Perry. Oscar Ward. Archie Brown. Elmer liked to fish; Oscar made elderberry wine; after 20 years of bachelorhood, Archie had married his high school sweetheart, a widow who with her two children had just moved back to Stone Valley. All three men, working together, had saved a boy from drowning, his body in shock after he dove into the cold waters of the quarry.

They're gone but Rose the corpse goes on, newspapers reserving their banner headlines and widest column space for her. Sex, murder, rape, tinder for a story burning hotter every day until it too finally flames out and another murdered woman takes Rose's place.

He pictured the owners of the major newspapers sitting on gold toilets in their estates built on granite and from there sending messages to their journalists about what to report. Fat rich men planning elaborate granite mausoleums for their bones while ignoring the death of three stone cutters. What was news? What sold. Lurid details about a pastor's wife.

Jones heard the three dead men laugh at him.

I know. I'm keeping the circus going by using you.

Not wanting to make Higgins suspicious, he'd lied saying he was looking for information about the accident.

What I want is a noose around someone's neck. That's all I can hope to control.

As he accelerated past the wagon, the car backfired, startling the two horses, the driver sitting on top of the logs fighting to control the team as the timber under him shifted. Jones stopped, jumped out, and shouting for the universe to hear: *"Elmer! Oscar! Archie!"* ran to grab the horses' harness.

* * *

Below the name BRAXTON MOTOR CO. painted in white letters across the top of a short, wide building, a large window festooned with American flag bunting showcased the black Ford parked inside. At each end of the building, a smooth stone pillar provided additional advertising space. On one, the business offered Polishing & Waxing, the other, Gasoline & Service, word, ampersand, word descending vertically down the columns.

Jones parked at the end of a row of new Model T's for sale and walked toward the entrance as a portly man wearing a derby too small for his big head and a suit, its vest buttons about to pop, hurried out the front door.

"Sheriff Jones! Happy to see you!" He shook Jones's hand "It's always a good day when I can help the law! Get you into something dependable—I know that's important in your line of work— but also spiffy! Have you thought about a sedan? Roomy and easy to drive. Electric starter, no more cranking! I have a few I can show you." He smiled, the shape perfect, his teeth glistening and bright.

"Actually, Mr. Braxton—"

"Monty, please."

"I want to show you something. The woman at the laundry said its yours."

"The one I lost! Where did you find it?'

"Around Rose Thornton's neck."

"Isn't that something, my kerchief used to strangle that poor woman." Braxton's face didn't lose its oily, plump jolliness. "I sold her husband his first car."

"When did you notice this missing?"

"Can't say. I have others, all silk like this one. I would like it back."

"Sure enough, once I find the murderer and he's hanged. Nellie Porter told me you left a motorcar at her house."

"A young man came in here Saturday thinking about buying a car. I showed him around and there was one he liked. He didn't have time to take it for a test drive but could that night. He was going to Mrs. Porter's. I agreed, said I'd drop it off and leave the ignition key with her."

"Did you know him?"

"He was just someone off the street. But if people don't walk in, I can't sell them a car!"

"Weren't you worried he'd steal it?"

"Trusting people is my biggest fault, Sheriff, that doesn't mean I'm a fool. The car's used but worth five hundred dollars. I left just enough gasoline in the tank for a short ride. There aren't many places where you can buy gas in Stone Valley—I wasn't going to sell it to him, that's for sure, and when I let Bill at Sauser hardware, old man Caputo in the General Store, and the pharmacist know what I was doing, they all agreed this fella wouldn't get any from them either. But maybe he did. When I picked the car up Sunday morning it had half a tank, a lot more than I'd put in."

"He must have given you his name."

"Butch Pratt, looked like a wolf. That didn't matter to me. I've had fancy white-haired ladies on the arm of their husbands walk around the lot, show interest in all the cars before telling me they preferred carriages. Then a farmer in dirty overalls will come in, go right to a truck, and pay for it in cash."

"You gave Mrs. Porter the key. Did you keep a spare?"

"Absolutely. You never know when you might lose something." A grin creased Braxton's jolly, fleshy face, but useless for business, quickly vanished.

"You could have driven the car late Saturday night."

"Depends what you mean by late. I'm in bed by nine, nine-thirty, get up early, have breakfast, then come here and make sure the cars are polished, in line, and ready for customers."

"Are you married, Mr. Braxton?"

"Unfortunately, never was."

"Lady friend?"

He laughed.

"I'm too old."

"Did you sell the car?"

"No, want to see it? It's out back."

Ice had formed at the bottom of the path shoveled alongside the building, FORD painted in 20-foot letters on the brick wall.

"Keep following me, Sheriff, I know where it's safe to walk. I'm as sure-footed as a goat!"

Sunlight through fog had warmed the black metal of the motor-cars parked in the rear lot, melting the snow covering them and exposing glistening, sunlit ice on car roofs.

"Beautiful, isn't it?" Braxton remarked and blew his nose.

"The car."

"Over there, by the milk truck."

Jones walked ahead, was looking inside the motorcar when Braxton caught up.

"I thought this was perfect for him, Sheriff. Curved front fenders, sleek black radiator and curved hood, a sporty looking automobile for a young man. And I gave him a good price. But instead of telling me he wasn't interested, which would have meant negotiating some more, he left the key and went his merry way. What a fine how-do-you-do after all I'd done to help him find the right car.

"Here's the good news, his mistake is your gain! I'll sell you this handsome, smoothly running machine that's only two years old and, hold on to your hat, can reach a top speed of *45 miles per hour*, for even a better deal than I offered Mr. Pratt. Four-Fifty and you'll drive away with a tank full of free gas. What do you say about that?"

"If I need anything else from you I'll let you know," Jones answered while continuing to search the car.

Confidentially walking on ice, Braxton headed back toward the showroom, slipped, arms flailing in the air as he fell backward, his derby flying off.

Using a magnifying glass and Dorcas's tweezers, Jones carefully picked up a few curly hairs and put them in an envelope. He found straight black strands, then a light brown one. He recognized the curl and knew how to identify the black hair, but the other?

Maybe Braxton's.

He watched the Ford dealer use both hands to pull his hat down as far as he could on his bald head.

A third person...

Finished inspecting the car's interior, Jones squatted near a tire and with a small brush inked the thread then pressed a sheet of white paper against the molded rubber. He compared the impression to the photograph taken of the tire marks on Winter Street near the murder scene. The same.

But there aren't that many choices in Stone Valley. Different cars can have the same kind of tires. Grange's matched too. What makes this one important is the hair.

"I've decided I want it," he informed Braxton, anxiously waiting in front of the building and ready to begin another sale's pitch.

"Excellent, Sheriff! You'll have dependable transportation for years! There's nothing like a Ford! About the price, I'm thinking I might have been too generous. I've gone over my costs, including having to wash and wax the vehicle after driving it back from Mrs. Potter's. I'm not talking about substantially more money, just—"

"Give me the ignition key, I'm impounding the car because it might have been used in the murder of Rose Thornton. The key—*now*." He planned to keep Braxton under 24-hour surveillance.

Jones did like the way the car accelerated, leaving Braxton standing with his hands pressed against his mouth.

Bordered on one side by vertically sliced mountains glittering with ice crystals and on the other, a 100-foot drop onto granite ledges, the road winding up from the valley required focused drivers.

Jones sped along while thinking about the case.

Rose Thornton was at the party house Saturday night where—

She talked to Buster Pratt.

Had a date with George Higgins.

It's only two blocks, a four-minute walk, from Porter's to the Bijou. If she was there a few minutes after 11 as the note I read said that means she left the Porter's house around 11.

Did Pratt or Higgins go with her?

Robbed, murdered, her body violated, all in the Colton Garden.

No one forced her into the yard.

She was strangled with a rope and Montgomery Braxton's handkerchief.

He has no way of proving he lost it and no verifiable alibi for where he was Saturday night.

An unfaithful wife, Rose had met many men at those supper parties. Any of them could have killed her.

I need more names.

I have three hair samples.

I'll visit the cemetery.

Tire marks on the car left in Porter's backyard match the ones on Winter Street.

So did Grange's.

Rose was naked except for her gloves and shoes.

Her clothes were neatly piled beside her.

She kicked trying to get away, was choked to death, then raped.

Grange found her lying face down.

The murderer was in no hurry. He robbed her and put her clothes in order. Why did he leave the shoes and gloves on?

Did he turn Rose over to rape her?

At home on Saturday she had dinner with the family at 5:30.

Time of death between 11 and 12:30.

Food was found in her stomach, probably meat.

Gillespie also stated he estimates she ate sometime between two to fours hours before her death. The earliest then would be seven.

At that Saturday night supper, Porter served only eggs, vegetables, and pudding.

Rose had a second meal.

With who?

The killer?

Does Pastor Thornton know his wife was one of Porter's regular date women?

How could he not know.

And if he does, why would this supposedly righteous crusader for virtue let his wife become a Saturday night sporting woman?

The car skidded on loose gravel toward the granite below. Jones turned away.

* * *

Its nature gloomy, a graveyard would seem the perfect place for fog to live, or if not that, picnic there on droplets seasoned with the smell of decay. Perhaps fog thought its talent unappreciated in the Stone Valley cemetery, that it found more satisfaction, could express itself better, by shrouding living people rather than drifting with innocuous blandness over rotting corpses and bones unimpressed by something that attempted to create creepiness by using condensed water.

"Dig us up and you'll see real horror," the dead said, "a graveyard of young men. We inhaled crystalline silica in the dust from pneumatic drills quarry owners gave us so we could work faster. Stone cutters' tuberculosis, they called it. Coughing, pain in the chest, then we couldn't breathe. The doctors said there were lumps of fibers on our lungs. We had wives. Children. Find them. Maybe they'll enjoy having you float over their graves."

But fog has no consciousness, and souls don't speak. Nor did the cemetery prevent the fog from infringing on the graveyard's ownership of the dead by using miasma from the decomposition of corpses to create a protective dome of noxious particles.

On this late afternoon, as Sheriff Jones walked toward the subterranean receiving vault built behind the burial ground, the thin old gravestones and the newer monuments of granite he passed radiated a cheerful brightness in the clear warm air simply because for today, sunlight had again managed to escape the fog.

The graveyard keeper had given him the key. After unlocking the iron gate, Jones descended stone slab steps, the temperature warmer than above ground, cooling as he stepped farther down, not as cold as the surface but sufficient for preserving the dead until graves could be dug in the Spring.

At the bottom of the granite chamber, the air moistureless and stale, Jones felt the ceiling only a few feet above his head and the bodies surrounding him on their shelves in the stone walls, press in, constricting space, making it hard for him to breathe. He saw men and women formed from shadows cast by a scattering of light from the vault's grated opening, standing, looking at him, unable to tell their stories. What they were—the joys, the pain, the hopes and desires—lost inside eternal silence.

But Rose would speak. He'd talk to her now.

Her casket stored, her body dressed in a burial gown, Jones slowly lifted the veil from her face. Eyes closed, mouth slightly open, formaldehyde had preserved her beauty. He smoothed her hair, compared it to the black strand he'd found.

They matched. He'd guessed right. On Saturday night, Rose Thornton had been in Braxton's motorcar.

At the funeral service, clamoring reporters had pushed and elbowed, knocked over flower arrangements and candles while trying to get a better photograph of Rose in her coffin. Jones had broken cameras and twisted arms, but he and his deputies had been unable to stop the outside world from further exploiting the death of a young mother who, although flawed, deserved to appear asleep in a room where her mourning family didn't have to kiss her goodbye in the harsh light from flash powder ignited by sweaty strangers.

She's not resting in peace even now.

Jones gently lowered her veil.

It was time to meet Grange at Mother Mae's.

"It's like he said, he came by bus. Here's what I got back from the chiefs." Grange handed Jones the telegrams. "Then there's this. We found it when searching his hotel room."

Jones ran inside and up the stairs, two at a time, unlocked the door and taking the startled boy by the neck shoved him against a wall, held him there while squeezing his throat.

"I'm going to enjoy watching you hang, you fucking coward. I'm sorry? I can't hear you. Are you trying to tell me that choking makes it hard to breathe?"

Pratt's eyes rolled back, his limp body sliding down the wall when Jones let go.

Although always wanting to save them, Grange knew when he

needed to spend a few extra heartbeats. He had reached the hallway as Jones entered the room and now didn't hesitate to pick Pratt up and drop him into a chair.

The sheriff noticed how easily his deputy lifted a body.

"Hand me that pitcher."

Jones poured water over Pratt's head. Coughing, the boy sat up, dizzy and terrified.

"You hear me, don't you? You know where you are?"

"Ye—yes," Pratt's managed to say, his voice a raspy whisper.

"Good. I wouldn't want your lawyer thinking you didn't have a clear head when confessing to murdering Rose Thornton. And if you confess, right now, to me, there's a chance, your only chance, you won't have to swing from a rope. You like supper parties? These are the appetizers for your necktie one.

"You ransacked a golf club in Rutland and ran off with a few silver-plated knives and a clock. Really, Pratt. You break into a place and that's what you take? But you did get more ambitious. In North-field you stole a ring and forged a check. Both towns have issued arrest warrants.

"You've admitted to meeting Mrs. Thornton. She was friendly and you liked how she looked.

"Taking the times you gave us, on your way back to the hotel you were on Winter Street at 11:48, which would be well within the one-and-a-half-hour range given by the corner as to when Mrs. Thornton died. You had an unaccounted for 13 minutes in your story.

"On Saturday, Montgomery Braxton left a Ford automobile at the Porter house because he thought you wanted to buy it. I have hair samples proving that you were in that car with Mrs. Thornton." Jones held the curly strand in front of Pratt's face. "But maybe I'm wrong." He yanked out a handful of Pratt's long beard, the young man screaming. "Calm down, boy, you won't miss it. Well look at this. Only difference, what I took now has a little blood on it.

"The tire tracks of the loaned vehicle and those found on Winter Street near the crime scene are identical. I have information that Sat-urday night, shortly after 11, Mrs. Thornton was standing outside the

Bijou. You had access to a motor car. This is what happened.

"As she continued to walk down Main Street toward her home, you offered her a ride. She liked you and got in. You drove to the Colton's where she made another mistake in a night of them. She went with you into that backyard. But then Mrs. Thornton changed her mind. Angry, lustful, you killed her and did more. I've timed it. The drive from North Main to the Colton yard takes seven minutes. A missing 13 minutes? Hell no! You had more time than that to enjoy yourself, return the car to the Porter house and walk back to the Arc, getting there at 12:05, just like you said. Know how I can prove all this? Our main course, the entrée that will put a noose around your neck."

Grange held up the wristwatch.

"Where did you find this, Deputy?"

"In Mr. Pratt's room, Sheriff."

"Bring it over to him, let him see the back. What's there, Pratt?"

"Initials. RP," He folded his arms across his chest, sat shaking and sweating.

"For Rose Prindle, Mrs. Thornton's maiden name, this watch a gift from a father to his daughter on her birthday, the beloved child you murdered."

"Wait! Sheriff! *Please*, I can explain!"

Jones laughed.

"How many times have I heard that! You'll get your chance in court. Then you'll hang."

"She was dead when I found her! I took the watch and her money, but I didn't kill her!"

"So you're admitting you're a thief who robs corpses. Then you have intercourse with them."

"*I'd never!*" Hands to his temples, eyes closed, he shouted the denial with the anguish of someone innocent or already damned.

"Look at me, goddamnit! Stop acting!" Jones grabbed Pratt by the hair and jerked his head up. "This isn't vaudeville and you're not some braying trained mule brought on stage for laughs!" He let go. "Tell me about the car you didn't mention when I questioned you before."

"I wanted to play the big shot, impress the girl I was going to meet by showing her I owned a motorcar, so I pretended I was interested in buying one and had the dealer drive it over to the Porter house. Hattie didn't want to go for a ride, so I drove around myself."

"When?"

"After ten."

"Anyone see you leave?

"People were in their rooms."

"What about Hattie? She'd know."

"She was with another man."

"How romantic.

"I thought it would be a good time to take the car out. I was back in a half-hour, left at 11:30, never saw Hattie again."

"You're quite the liar, Pratt. I see now why you lied to me before about being at the Porter house the whole evening. You'd used the car in a murder."

"That's not it, Sheriff—no—the car didn't have much gas, so I stole some. I thought you might know about the break-in at the hardware store and what was taken."

"I'd accused you of being a murderer and rapist and you were worried I'd arrest you for stealing gasoline?"

"That's something I did."

Pratt began crying. For a few moments, Jones stood looking at him.

"How old are you?"

"Eighteen."

"Shit, just a kid." Jones got a wet towel and handed it to Pratt. "Go on, wipe your face. You got any more of that Mary Jane candy you carry around?" he asked Grange.

"I do, Sheriff."

"Give him a piece." Jones sighed. "Damn, this case has gotten to me, turned me into real asshole. I'm not usually this way, am I Grange."

"No, Sheriff, you're not."

"I've been too harsh on you, Pratt, not really listening. I apologize. Maybe you are innocent, and I should help you. Do you know of anyone who could testify that from 10:30, the time you say you brought it back, until the next morning, the motorcar was parked in Porter's backyard?"

"Mrs. Porter. I returned the key."

"You gave it to her?"

"I put it on her desk."

"That doesn't help. But maybe I should look at the facts differently, in a more favorable light, one not leading to a death sentence. Motorcars can have the same brand tire. Mrs. Thornton's hair looks like the strand I found in the car but there are a lot of dark-haired women on the planet. And the wristwatch? You robbed a corpse on your way back to the hotel. You won't hang for that.

"If you admit that sometime between 11 pm Saturday, January 4 and 12:30 am Sunday, January 5, 1919, you were in the Colton backyard and when there robbed the corpse of Mrs. Rose Thornton, stealing her wristwatch, money, and wedding ring, I'll arrest you for theft. We can then put this whole unpleasant business behind us. You're too young and stupid to be executed for murder."

"OK, Sheriff Jones," Pratt said, resignation making his words barely audible. "Except for one thing. I didn't take the ring."

"We'll leave that out."

Grange wrote and dated the admission, gave it to Pratt to sign.

"Is this a true statement of facts?" Jones asked.

Pratt nodded.

"I need an answer."

"Yes, it's what happened."

"And you sign it of your own volition, meaning no one forced you?"

"I robbed her."

Pratt carefully, but in large, ill-formed letters, printed his name. Mother Mae witnessed.

Grange handed the paper to Jones.

"Butch Pratt, I hereby arrest you for theft—"

Pratt's face and body began to relax.

"—and for the rape and murder of Rose Thornton, resident of

the town of Stone Valley, state of Vermont."

"*No!*" Pratt leaped forward. Jones kneed him in the stomach, propelling him onto the chair that toppling backward carried Pratt crashing to the floor.

Grange and another deputy dragged him into the hall by his shoulders. Cuffed and gasping, he tried resisting by bending his legs.

"Stop fighting, son, all it'll do is make you sweat," Grange said, his voice as soft and low as when talking to his dolls. After helping Pratt up, they walked slowly down the stairs to the waiting police wagon, the boy a heavy defeated weight between the two officers.

"Thank you, Mother Mae," Jones said after paying her.

"I'm sorry I wasted good stew on him. Hangings too merciful. I'd tie each of his legs to a horse then bring out a snake." Her black dress, silver cross, and the pure white lace on her neck and head hadn't changed, but Mother Mae's not unkind eyes had darkened. Although never a mother, she again felt the joy of having delivered another man to Hell.

Jones had Mrs. Porter arrested, then before driving home to *Queen's End* called Prescott with the news.

"That's great, Sheriff, just great! You got him with four days to spare! I never doubted you could do it. Bor might have, but what does he know about a person like you? He's very good at what he does—hurries over to empty my spittoon, goes into town if someone needs reminding who I am and what I expect, but he's no student of human nature. He's a goddamn mute! For me, people are like tools in a shed, each useful in different ways. When I'm hard on you, Sherriff, it's because I want to motivate your ass, not because I think you're not capable of doing what I want done.

"We have our murderer! My banner headline tomorrow will scoop all the Boston newspapers with their Jew-boy reporters: Killer Caught! Out-of-Towner Responsible For Murder of Pastor's Wife! Couldn't be better if I planned it myself! A dirty drifter comes into our city, he murders and rapes a woman he met who shouldn't have been whoring around, and in three days we have him in jail, waiting to be hanged."

Jones heard the hiss of expelled spit.

"I told you to arrest Nellie Porter, the whoremonger responsible for all this. Why did you wait?"

Jones knew what he'd see if in Perkins's office with him—threatening, red-tinged eyes in a crinkling red face.

"I thought she could still be useful. People talk if they're afraid of getting arrested. She wasn't going anywhere."

"Her house?"

"No longer a South End business."

"I'll make up for the loss by charging the others an additional five percent. Let them know when you're there collecting on Sunday that this increase is just the first. Prohibition's coming. That's good for everyone. Liquor sales will double and what do drunk men want? Women! Tell the bar owners and madams that you'll continue protecting their business interests but protection from the Feds costs money. It's only fair. If they make more, so should we. They'll understand.

"You'll be sitting pretty, Sheriff, have enough of those silver dollars you save to buy a nice house. I can see it now, your lovely Dorcas in the kitchen baking cookies. Maybe you'll have me over for dinner!"

"Thank you, Mr. Perkins, but I like where I live."

"That's understandable. It's convenient. You have everything you need."

"If we wait to arraign Pratt, I'll have a few extra days to tie up some loose ends."

"I thought this was settled."

Again, not just coldness in his voice, but recrimination and lurking just below that, reprisal.

"Paperwork, that's all. Nothing to worry about." Jones immediately regretted saying it.

"Hear that Bor? Sheriff Jones is cradling us in his arms."

The giant slammed his fist against the wall, the sound and its message clearly heard over the telephone line.

"He's more articulate than most people who can talk. I never worry, Jones, and I always win. No delays! I'll call Wheeler, have the judge schedule Pratt's arraignment for Monday along with Porter's. They'll need a lawyer, can't think of a better one than Donald Duffins. Last man he represented went to prison for stealing chickens. I'll pay his fee.

"Yes, Sheriff, really great! Continue keeping Stone Valley safe!"

The conversation over, Jones felt as unclean as he did when in Perkins's office and needing to wash his face in rabbit blood.

* * *

At the wide scarred planks nailed into empty rum barrels, the counter stained with blood from fights and the sweat of drunken, used up men and women, Jones sat and finished his beer. He knew Dorcas did her best to keep the bar clean. She used vinegar and olive oil on the wood, polished the few remaining pieces of brass, wiped the black-spotted mirror hanging over gin and whiskey bottles, and mopped, her foot stopping the soap bucket from sliding down the sloping floor. But some stains were too deep to get out.

"I won't be going up with you tonight," Jones told her.

"That's fine, Sheriff. I know you're tired." She brought him another beer.

Back straight, broad shouldered and tall, his skin smooth and black, the man walked to the counter and sat down, Jones watching him. So did a whore with torn stockings and four grizzled men playing poker for pennies.

"What can I get you?" Dorcas asked.

"Whiskey." He put two-bits on the counter, continued looking in the mirror.

"You like to see who's behind you, that's smart," Jones said.

"I do, Sheriff," the man answered without turning his head.

"Military?"

"369 Infantry." He faced Jones. "How can you tell?"

"A lot of soldiers come through here. They have a certain look."

"Especially in the eyes. But I'm not sure about you. Did you serve?"

"I registered. The local draft board thought a sheriff is needed in town."

"Would you have gone?"

"If drafted."

"But not enlist. May I ask why?"

"I'm not a young man and it wasn't my war. An archduke got shot, countries picked sides, and men began dying. There's a big ocean between us and the Germans. They weren't coming here."

"Talking like that could have put you in prison."

"I waved a flag, just like everyone else. Did you join up?"

"To get women. All it takes is a uniform." Old eyes, he didn't smile. "Sheriff Jones, I know you have a reputation for keeping an orderly town. I'm just passing through. My name is Grant, Asa Grant."

"Lady killer."

"Sergeant. But I was popular in France. The mademoiselles dated Negro soldiers, found us more interesting than white ones, southern boys spreading the rumor we had tails. The French women wanted to see if that was true. For the first time in my life, I was in a country where I wouldn't get hanged for talking to a white woman."

"Maybe you should have stayed there."

"I fought for freedom."

"That's why we got into it, right? Wilson's big slogan, make the world safe for democracy."

"Not the world but here, for Negroes. We're still fighting."

"That's disturbing for a policeman to hear."

"I won't cause you any trouble."

"But I'm interested in what you said. The liquor's cheap. I've got time."

"If I don't?"

"That wouldn't be friendly," Jones answered.

Grant took his drink. Jones followed him to a table.

"Maybe we should play poker. I've got a few dollars."

"I'm not much of a card player, Mr. Grant. Never learned how to bluff."

A trace of a smile, then Grant finished his whiskey.

"When Congress declared war, black men wanted to prove to whites that if given the chance we would fight with courage. Does that sound strange to you, that a person would be willing to die in order to be respected?"

"No. Most times death has no meaning at all."

"But Negroes, enlisted or drafted, were placed in non-combative service battalions. The 369 was one of the exceptions. Under French command we fought in the second battle of the Marne and the Meuser-Argonne offensive. One hundred and seventy of us received the Croix de Guerre medal for bravery."

"Were you one of them?"

"I might have it someplace. We thought that because of our service, our blood sacrifice, the white world would accept us as equals. Instead, they saw the fighting Negro as a threat to white supremacy. Any lynching sends a message, but when you see a black man in uniform hanging from a tree you know as a returning black soldier you fought for a lie."

"Never been in the South," Jones said. "Don't think I'd like it."

"What about the North, Sheriff? No one in a white neighborhood will sell to a Negro family. Negroes live where they can, crowded together and isolated in cities within white cities, residential segregation with no way out. The South now has laws enforcing segregation but during slavery plantation owners had close contact with their slaves. The idea of separating blacks from whites was a Northern one. In Massachusetts, Negroes were physically prevented from sitting in a white only railroad car. The Pennsylvania Supreme Court ruled that businesses have a right to separate the races, the case before it that of a black woman, a teacher, who refused to ride in the colored only section of a train."

"The world isn't perfect, Mr. Grant."

"Seems to work just fine if you're white. I don't see many black faces in Stone Valley."

"There's five. The men are stone cutters."

"Five."

"Quarry jobs are hard to get."

"Especially if you're a Negro."

"You said I have a reputation. It's earned. Stone Valley is a peaceful town and I intend to keep it that way. There are people living here who *are* troublemakers. Quarry workers wanting better working conditions unionize and are either striking or threatening to walk off the job. We have socialists, the burn down city hall type and the ones who want to take over by getting voted in. There's anarchists and moral crusaders."

"Don't forget the Ku Klux Klan."

"They gather in a barn and have more cows at their meetings than members. I'm not worried about them. But the others? Like a man who sits in a bar and talks about still fighting for freedom. That's someone I need to watch."

"Tomorrow I'll be gone."

"Where are you staying, Mr. Grant?"

"Where they'll have me. South End boarding house."

"Don't check out. There's been a murder."

"I read about it. Black man no one knows, white woman dead, of course I'm a suspect. I arrived yesterday, you can ask the landlady. The murder was Sunday, wasn't it?"

"Or Saturday night and you could have been in Stone Valley before that. I'm not accusing you of anything but until this case is solved, I'll need you available for questioning. A couple of days, that's all. Like you said, you're a stranger."

In Grant's eyes, Jones saw the defiance of a man who if unable to live free would choose to die.

"I have a knife, Sheriff Jones," Grant stated calmly.

"I saw it when you came in. I treat people fairly and this *isn't* the South. Don't run. That would be a mistake. Dorcas, bring Sergeant Grant another whiskey."

Jones paid for it and left.

Earlier, hazy twilight through Dorcas's fog-stained window coated her walls and splashed her bed and end table with the tired glow of spent fire, the room becoming with night small grey-tone shadows hiding and reappearing as if playing peek-a-boo with a baby summoned by memory from the dead. Dorcas always lit a candle before entering.

Two floors below, in Jones's windowless room, the animal pelts hanging along the walls had disappeared into the thick darkness pressing down on him with the weight of entombing silence. Stretched out, his feet overhanging the bed, he closed his eyes, his breathing slowing as the dark, becoming even blacker, sealed him in. Jumbled thoughts died leaving only the ones that grew in dead bodies.

I have Pratt.

Braxton, Grange, now the Negro, are on shelves.

George Higgins.

The hair. The car.

He slept without dreaming.

6

Thursday Day Four

"Sheriff!"

"One pose! In front of the station!"

"With Pratt!"

"You and Rose's corpse!"

Jones pushed through the gaggle of reporters, press cameras ready, all wanting photographs for half-tone printing in their newspapers of Bull Gideon Jones, the local sheriff who had captured the killer of Rose Thornton, the story one of betrayal, infidelity, and acts so unspeakable common decency required reporting them with sensitivity for the feelings of readers while still giving them all the salacious facts.

A deputy let Jones in and quickly closed the police station door. "The jail?"

"They know. Only the lawyer." Grange answered from his desk.

"Not even him. Call Duffins. We'll tell him when he can see Pratt."

"Yes, Sheriff." Grange put his fork down, slowly closed the lid on his can of sardines.

Ahead, in his office, Jones saw Shapiro waiting for him.

"Who took his money?" Not pretending to wait for an answer he knew he wouldn't get, Jones left the deputies, all of them, except Grange, suddenly looking very busy.

"Guess you didn't need me to make you a star, you've done that yourself. The *Gazette* gets the scoop and our big city newspapers look like rags. Roscoe Perkins and you must be good friends."

"Whenever I need a partner for whist."

"Business partnership too?"

"I'm the sheriff. He owns a newspaper. No connection."

"I'm planning on looking into that too."

Jones cracked his knuckles. He found the few grey curls in Shapiro's black hair particularly loathsome. Out of place, they detracted from the reporter's handsome, though thin-lipped face. Jones wanted simplicity; a man's character shown by his physical appearance. Even Shapiro's limp made him annoying, the impediment not preventing him from speeding along in his effort to uncover secrets.

He chased a storyline, that Rose was murdered in Porter's house. Now he's back on track and with more fish to fry, Perkins and me.

"Sometimes, when I was younger, I worried about the unexpected," Jones began. "I'd be out walking, enjoying the day, maybe thinking about hunting or fishing or how warm it was for October, when suddenly I'd stop and look around, worried that someone might walk over, smile, and shoot me. I'd be gone, in an instant. Ever wonder about that sort of thing, Mr. Shapiro? I'm only asking because like me, you have a dangerous job."

"I'm after the story, Sheriff, nothing else matters. Stone Valley has a street of churches, two blocks of saloons and bordellos and sometime last weekend a churchwoman was raped and murdered here. For a reporter, this place is the promised land."

"Moses didn't get to see it."

"But God loves the truth and you're the law. What could happen."

"Not stopping that one person with a gun."

"Who you no longer worry about. What can you tell me about Pratt?"

"Nothing."

"The *Gazette* reported he was in the Colton yard when Mrs. Thornton was robbed and murdered. Do you have evidence proving that?"

"You'll find out at the trial."

"Did he rob her first?"

"Same answer."

"Why was Nellie Porter arrested?"

"She's an accessory to murder."

"I don't understand. If the crime took place at the Colton's how is Porter involved? Is that why her house is boarded up?"

"Mrs. Porter has also been charged with operating a house of ill repute."

"Like the other ones in the South End."

"Hers was unlicensed, unregulated, and had numerous health code violations. The other businesses you refer to generate significant tax revenue for the city and are professionally run."

"May I talk to Pratt?"

"No."

"Porter?'

"I'm afraid not."

"Have they hired attorneys?"

"Don't know. So, if that's all, I'd like my office back."

Shapiro paused at the door.

"When's the arraignment?"

"Monday."

"Why not today?"

"Judge Wheeler probably has a busy schedule."

"Lots of murdered women on his docket?'

"Good day, Mr. Shapiro."

Jones looked at the clock.

Two hours before Higgins, enough time to get this done.

The Stone Valley Church of Christ, it's only adornment the iron cross at the apex of a gray wooden steeple, the rest of the building faded brick, the snow and cold of Vermont having created a dull but unform looking exterior, achieving in this way what the church's founders had wanted when washing the brick with red iron oxide, no variation in color.

Long and narrow rectangular windows had been designed to let in more shadows than light. To enter, Jones had to push hard on the heavy front door.

Walls without paintings or symbols, the pews in the nave faced a 20-foot cross, the floors smooth cold rocks. As Jones climbed toward Thornton's office in the loft, he remembered why he had once attended services here with Dorcas. The architecture, the setting, didn't inspire belief, it presented order, sermons in stone. It asked congregants to sit and listen to their Shepherd, pastors who in each generation reaffirmed dogma unchanged since the church's founding.

Dorcas had found comfort in these absolutes. Jones had too, until their daughter died.

He'd asked Thornton why.

"God wanted her. She's His newest angel."

Jones heard the words but what he saw was Thornton's eyes, dark and as cold as the church's stone floors.

"Pastor."

At his desk in an office with non-perpendicular angles he'd tried to make into a standard, rectangular shaped room by hanging folds of black cloth on wires, Thornton looked up from his Bible.

"More questions, Sheriff? You've caught the murderer. What else is there to know?"

"It's about your wife."

Thornton folded his arms.

"Go on."

"Out of respect for you and your children, the *Gazette* didn't report what I found out about Mrs. Thornton. I'm sorry I'm the one who has to tell you. On Saturday nights she dated men she met at Nellie Porter's house. Pratt was there. That's how he knew her. There are reporters still snooping around and the trial will be public. Eventually everyone will know."

Thornton sat back, tapped his finger on the Bible.

"Surprising."

"Shocking, actually."

"I'm surprised how well you play your role. You express just the right amount of concern for my feelings. Very professional. I've always known where Rose went on Saturday nights."

"That means you lied to me."

"Why tell you the truth?"

"I was investigating a murder."

"And I have children to protect. I prayed for Rose, counseled her, blessed her as she knelt, my hand on her head. I hoped she'd repent and find her way back to Jesus, ask for his forgiveness and be reborn, maybe actually go to the picture show and come home. I gave her money. She spent it on candy.

"I believe in the sanctity of marriage. It is an unbreakable commitment before God. I couldn't divorce Rose, but I could find peace in my own heart by fighting against the sin in this city, the moral corruption and decay the devil and his minions have spawned to ensnarl weak women like my wife.

"I loved Rose and I know she loved me. She'd ask for my forgiveness and I'd give it, but I'm not God. He's given us free will and the choices she made were her own. When she died a part of me did too because I could no longer pray and hope for her salvation. Those with knowledge of the Holy Spirit who reject Christ's love are damned."

"You told your children she was in heaven."

"Better to give her wings and make her one of God's angels than tell them the truth. She is burning in hell."

Wings and angels, words for children and fathers with dead babies from this holy man self-contained within his shell of piety.

"I'll pray for you too, Sheriff." Thornton went back to reading his Bible.

In his car, Jones looked down at his hands and remembering how small his daughter had looked in them, how protective of her he'd felt, he cursed a non-existent God.

* * *

"Mr. Higgins?"

"Yes sir."

A skinny man with a carefully positioned curl above one eye, he wore a brown wool suit with cuffs and three cuff buttons, begonia purple tie, stick pin, red pocket square, and black brogue shoes. Lubricant oil had stained his fingers.

They shook hands.

"I appreciate you stopping by."

"No problem, Sheriff."

They went into Jones's office.

"Please, have a seat." Jones went behind his desk, Higgins sat in front, grinning and looking around.

"I like the moose head. That was a big animal."

"Over 1200 pounds."

"You shoot it?"

"I did. Do you hunt?"

"No, never liked the idea of killing something. No offense intended, Sheriff."

"None taken, Mr. Higgins. So, about the accident."

"Bad luck for those boys. They knew their job but that's what it's like in the quarry. You get up, have breakfast, go to work, think everything's fine then something happens that's not your fault and you end up dead. I only know what I heard. I was working a different shift."

"Well, since you're here, maybe we can chat about something else."

"Sure, Sheriff, whatever you like."

"Did you know Rose Thornton?"

"Never met the woman."

"Your wife did."

"Probably from church. I don't go. I know who she was, of course, 'cause like I said, word gets around and when you're 300 feet down in a quarry hole there can be a lot of talking, mostly about women."

"Dead ones?"

"Good one, Sheriff," and Higgins laughed.

"You must have read about the murder."

"I don't read. Well, I do, a little, but the only thing I like in a newspaper is the comic *Krazy Kat.*

"Nellie Porter—you know her, of course."

"Hm, Nellie Porter, maybe... yes."

"On Saturday nights you've gone to her house."

"For supper, if you can call it that."

"I wouldn't. You meet women there for sex."

"I'd be lying if I said they weren't interested in me." Eyes brightening, he tilted his head slightly, compressed his lips into a cocky smile.

"Porter told me one of them was Mrs. Thornton, that you had a date with her last Saturday."

"She said that? Then I guess I did."

"Was it the first time?"

"Definitely! First time."

"Porter thought it was more like the fourth."

"She's probably right."

"Did you have intercourse with Mrs. Thornton on those occasions?"

"I'm married, Sheriff! You met my wife. Very pretty gal, don't you think? OK, I did."

"Meaning Saturday too?"

"Yessir." He coughed into his pocket square, folded it neatly back into his breast pocket.

"Can you tie a square knot?"

"Easy as pie," Higgins answered.

Jones handed him the three-foot length of rope. Higgins quickly knotted it.

"Want a clove hitch too?"

"No, this'll do." Jones put the ligature into his desk drawer. "On Saturday nights you had sexual relations with women Porter introduced you to, one of them Mrs. Thornton. Weren't you afraid your wife would find out?"

"She doesn't mind."

"Really? I'd say you're married to a very understanding woman."

"I met Hazel and bought a mule the same year. Mule's dead but Hazel's still with me ten years later so I must be doing something right. She makes dinner, we play cards, do it a few times a week, and I keep working in the pit. Saturdays I plug about but she knows it's just for fun, that I'm not leaving her for some floozie."

"Is that what Mrs. Thornton was to you?"

"No sir. She was a preacher's wife."

"You wear your hair long."

"Long, conditioned with Macassar oil and brushed into place. I have hair like my pop and granddaddy. I come from a family of men with wavy blond hair. It's a blessing."

"Actually, the color's more sandy brown than blond. Like this, wouldn't you say?" Jones showed him the hair he'd taken from the Braxton motorcar.

"Isn't that something. Could have come from my brush."

"How did you get to Mrs. Porter's?"

"Sometimes trolly, sometimes car. It depends on how long I'm staying."

"Last Saturday?"

"Drove."

"You planned to stay late."

"Hoped to."

"You parked at Porter's—"

"No, a block over at Pinky's. I had a few drinks there, then walked to the house."

"Where you continued your affair with Mrs. Thornton."

"We had sex, like I've said. More than once that night," Higgins stated proudly.

"Who left first?"

"She did."

"What time?"

"Around 11."

"You saw the time on one of the clocks in the house?"

"I have a watch." He swung it out from his fob pocket. "All brass."

"When did you get home?"

"A little after 12."

"I found the hair I showed you in a car that on Saturday night was parked in the Porter backyard. I'd like a sample of yours."

"*Cut my hair.*"

"A small piece. I'll have an expert examine both to see if they match."

"They can do that?"

"Police use evidence like this all the time. It's foolproof."

"Am I in trouble?"

"Of course not. Just curious as to why you were in that car when you had your own parked nearby."

"Maybe I was acting like a little kid, sitting behind the wheel and pretending to drive."

"You want me to believe that?"

"You could. I clown around a lot, just ask Hazel. Here's what happened. It was a nifty Ford so I took it for a spin."

"Where did you get the car key?"

"Seen a fella at the house—beaver type, long beard, straggly hair he didn't try to brush smooth—take a key from on top of Mrs. Porter's desk. I'm curious too, so I followed him out back and watched him drive off."

"When was this?"

"Around 10:00."

"That matches what Pratt told me."

"He returned a little before 12."

"He said 10:30."

"Then he's wrong. I kept checking the time, hoping he'd get back before I had to leave. I wasn't going to stay past 12 and pay extra for nothing. He left the key, I took it, and had my little ride. Real nice motor car."

"Where did you go?"

"Around the block, that's it."

"Anyone see you?'

"The drunks at Pinky's. After parking the car, I got mine and went straight home."

"Hazel will vouch for that?"

"You bet! She was waiting and we went to bed."

"Weren't you worried you were driving away in someone's car?"

"Nope. Above the license plate in back there was a smaller steel one that had Owned by the Braxton Motor Car Company stamped into it. The car was a loaner, and I was doing what was expected.

Borrowing it."

"You didn't like the suppers at Mrs. Porter's?"

"They're great, if you're a rabbit. Not one bit of meat. I'd usually go out and buy something."

"Did you Saturday?"

"Got sausages from Big Max at the South End butcher shop. He has this red sausage machine. Minced meat goes in with his special seasonings, skin on the nozzle, and he turns the handle. After tying up the individual sausages that come out on a string, he cuts them off. Saturday, he cut off two. One for me, one for Rose."

"She ate with you?"

"I wouldn't have gone to Big Max's place without her. She was hungry too and I'm a gentleman. Sheriff, may I ask you something."

"Sure, Mr. Higgins, go right ahead."

"You're asking me a lot of questions about Saturday night. Don't you already have the murderer in jail? It seems like you're trying to measure my neck for that noose. Not that I'm worried. I didn't kill anyone and I'm always willing to cooperate with the law except the time Clyde Smithers sliced off a piece of the pork belly I was smoking. I took care of it, taught him that he shouldn't take what I would have given him if he'd only asked. Didn't bother you about it, Sheriff, and he never troubled me again."

"We have arrested the man responsible for the death of Rose Thornton. I just wanted to fill in a few of the missing pieces. You have been very helpful."

"Glad I could do it!" Higgins coughed, took a few deep breaths, still breathing hard after standing up. "Silicosis. I'm dying. Comes with the job. A 1200-pound moose. How many times did you have to shoot it?"

"Just once."

"One bullet. You wouldn't think that'd be enough."

He left, and Jones leaned back in his chair.

With Pratt in custody, I hoped Higgins would be less guarded and in a strange way, he was. He lied, then admitted knowing Rose and having had sex with her multiple times. He changed his answers but was very clear about his timeline regarding the Braxton car. He went for a short ride around midnight, drove home in his own car, and got into bed with his wife. But Pratt, according to Higgins's story, drove that motorcar from ten until almost 12. He said he doesn't read the newspapers. Should I believe that? Think it's just a coincidence that his timeline puts Pratt in the murder car at an hour when, according to the papers reporting the coroner's findings as to time of death, Rose Thornton could have been murdered?

Higgins wants Pratt hanged.

Does that make George Higgins the murderer or someone who thinks he's a Casanova and still resents Pratt because Rose liked him?

I could destroy Higgins's credibility by telling the jury about all the lies he told when I questioned him.

I could testify that based on the hair I found, Rose was inside the Braxton car with either Pratt or Higgins driving but only Higgins knew how to quickly tie a square knot.

As for Pratt admitting he was in the Colton backyard when Rose was murdered, maybe I'll confess to having tricked him into signing the statement.

Higgins might hang, but what if he isn't the murderer? What if there were other stands of hair from other men in that car, I just didn't find them?

If Higgins did it, why? Was it premeditated? Rose knew something about him and he killed her to keep her quiet, the rape just for fun, his terminal illness removing all moral restraints?

Is he really dying?

Are there enemies of Thornton in the mix?

In all this, what becomes of Pratt?

He called Doctor Foster's house, spoke to his secretary, Mrs. Foster, and finding out from her that the doctor had just left on a house call, got the address.

Tired and grumpy, his clothes as disarranged as his white hair, Foster peered over the top of his glasses while impatiently drumming his fingers on the dented hood of his old car.

"It's privileged. Period. You should know that. You're making me late."

"He already told me. I'm just confirming it."

"And if I tell you it's not true, I'm divulging medical information about a patient."

"Who would have lied to me in a police investigation."

"It's progressing. His wife will become one more of Stone Valley's destitute widows. Goddamn weather, makes my bones ache and you can't see shit!"

Battered medical bag in hand, he hurried away, cursing the cold and fog.

* * *

Behind him on a stage built in front of the Old Town Hall and hanging in rigid folds from ten-foot poles, five U.S. flags alternated with five flags of the Civic Council, its purity movement symbol a purple cross on a white field.

To one side of the stage, a large sign pictured a woman dressed in the style of ancient Greece, rectangular fabric folded around her body, holding a banner above her head:

Stop White Slave Traffic

Printed at her feet, words on a long curving ribbon,

The Appeal of Womanhood

At the stage's other end, Mankind's Future, and its eugenics tree stood beside a placard calling for the end of birth control.

Passionate reformers committed to restoring social purity by advocating for laws based on Christian values, women with babies and children, husbands in tow, reporters, and a scattering of workmen, waited for Pastor Thornton to speak.

Twilight through wisps of fog colored him and those below in rolling waves of simmering crimson brightening with the dying sun.

Jones stood in the shadow of the old building.

"My wife was a sinner," Thornton stated quietly, his reddening dark form as straight and stiff as the flags and flagpoles behind him. "We all are. Jesus died for us. I have accepted him as my savior. Many of you have also welcomed Christ into your life. For us, given by grace, there is redemption. Through the atoning sacrifice of our Lord upon the cross, we are saved. But for others, even if baptized, attend church, and speak the words of the righteous, they do not, by their actions and in their hearts, believe in Jesus Christ. They have not humbled themselves before him. These people are Christians in name only. Their sins are not forgiven. My wife was one of them."

Thornton spoke more forcefully.

"What awaits the lustful, the drunken, the lost among us who, like my beloved wife, the mother of my children, die unrepentant? Eternal damnation. The fires of Hell. I stand before you a failure. I prayed, I tried, but I could not lead her back to the path of righteousness. God has given us free will and the pull of this," he pointed a long, stake-like finger toward the South End, "was too strong, Satan's hold on her too great." Thornton glanced down, spoke as if to himself, everyone able to hear. "Her body that was once God's temple, defiled, and lying on a bed of ice."

He looked up and for a moment his severe features seemed less angular, his straight posture slightly stooped. Then his eyes cleared.

"I no longer have a wife nor my children a mother. When reporters write about Rose, they write the words of this world. I wanted you to know the spiritual truth. There is Heaven and there is Hell, and though my faith has been tested, I will not give up! I will not let the devil win! Our moral crusade goes on!"

"Amen!" many in the audience yelled. "Glory to God!"

The reporters took notes.

"As president of the Civic Council, as pastor of the Stone Valley Church of Christ, I have spoken and preached about the cancer in our city that is destroying virtue, morality, and the very image of God in us. The misery and degradation in the South End reach into our homes with disease, violence, infidelity, drunkenness, and now murder.

"But do not despair. Our fight has borne fruit. Prohibition is law, we've raised the age of consent to 16, and because of the Mann Act, evil men who defile the purity of women will be caught and imprisoned. We are building a better, more God-fearing society by legislating morality but there is more work to be done.

"We were made in the image of God. When we breed like animals the race of man is polluted. Let you, the physically and mentally strong, have large families. It is your duty. Contraception should be banned except for those unfit to reproduce.

"The Bible condemns prostitution. Paul said, 'Do you not know that your bodies are members of Christ? Shall I then take the members of Christ and make them members of a prostitute? Never!'"

Thornton's voice became progressively louder.

"Should we let prostitutes infect unsuspecting wives with venereal diseases?

"Should we let prostitutes tear families asunder?

"Should businessmen in Stone Valley earn filthy lucre by creating perverted Edens where women again tempt men to sin?

"*I say no*! Now is not the time for us to wait for the Federal government to close the saloons or make prostitution illegal. We need to end corruption in Stone Valley, vote for those who protect, not exploit! Cleanse the temple! Put the money lenders in jail!"

Cheers, clapping, the waving of signs, torches lighting the night, the flames directed at the South End.

On the crowd's perimeter, men hired by Roscoe Perkins moved a little closer, metal batons ready. Violent and effective, gathered from impoverished, rural parts of Vermont, they acted as Perkins's enforcers. When quarry owners wanted to force stone cutters back to work, they paid him. Strikes in Stone Valley were bloody, but they never lasted more than a week.

Accompanied by two police officers carrying pump-action shotguns, Jones walked on stage.

"Thank you, Pastor Thornton, for your spiritual guidance and ideas on how to make our city better," he said while looking out toward the crowd. "Now it's time to reopen the street. This rally is over."

The armed deputies stepped forward.

Those who Thornton had just inculcated with religious fervor, quieted into silence. Torches dropped and smoldering out, signs left behind, the gathering dispersed, most of the women singing hymns while marching toward home.

"I'm surprised you let me finish," Thornton said as he and Jones left the stage.

"Freedom of speech, Pastor."

"While surrounded by Perkins's goons."

"Mr. Perkins has the right to give men jobs and use them where he chooses. They didn't break the law."

"Or intimidate me. I will continue speaking truth to Caesar."

"Free speech and free will. Your decision to make."

"See you in church, Sheriff."

He walked away, disappearing into the fog.

"Sheriff Jones."

"Mrs. Higgins. You shouldn't still be out here. Where's Mr. Higgins?"

"At home."

"I'll give you a ride to the station. You can call him from there."

"There's something you should know about George." Her hair no longer pulled back into a bun, blonde curls framed her face, her grey-blue eyes clear and direct. "He told me he killed Mrs. Thornton."

"He confessed? To murdering her?"

"This morning, after you met, instead of going to work he went drinking. He came home drunk, started crying and said what he'd done."

"Why would he tell you?"

"He felt guilty."

"Did he rape her too?"

"No. It was rough sex that got out of hand and when she resisted, he strangled her. "

"She'd been violated."

"Isn't confessing to murder enough."

"Why should I believe you?"

"I have no reason to lie."

"You have reason enough. Revenge. Your husband is a philanderer. He was having an affair with Rose Thornton."

Her doll-like lips parted in a small smile.

"George is weak. I've accepted that."

"Perjury's a crime, Mrs. Higgins."

"I met George when I was 18. He's four years older than me. He was selling Bibles door-to-door and came to our house. I still have the one my mother bought from him. He asked her if he could take me out for ice cream. George dressed nicely and was polite. She said yes. He bought the ice cream at the carnival. We rode the Ferris wheel and when reaching the top, he kissed me.

"I loved him then, I love him now, I will always love George Higgins. But I'll go to the police station tonight and repeat under oath what he told me about murdering Mrs. Thornton. How can I let a murderer go unpunished, live a normal life as if he'd done nothing wrong. There's an innocent young man in jail for murder. But I know, after I do this, I'll never be the same."

"You're a brave woman, Mrs. Higgins. From what you've just said I'd arrest him if I could."

"It'll be easy enough. He's passed out on our couch."

"A jury would never hear about the confession. A wife can't testify against her husband."

"George and I aren't married. He never wanted to and now I understand why. God had a plan for me. I've lived in sin for a purpose."

"OK, then, we'll bring him in."

"He's sick. Maybe he'll die before he's hanged. I'd like that." She closed her eyes as if praying, opened them, their gray-blueness softened by sadness, regret, or something else, Jones couldn't tell. "I don't want to stay in that house."

"You won't have to. I'll make arrangements with Mother Mae."

"Thank you." She walked ahead of him toward his car.

* * *

Hazel had been right. He didn't resist.

"Are we having a party?" Higgins's words slurred as Grange and another deputy helped him stand, stopped him from falling back onto the couch. "Hazel! Make me and the boys here some sandwiches.

Handcuffs? Sheriff! I thought we were pals!"

"I'm arresting you for the murder of—"

"I know! Rose! Beautiful, dark-haired Rose! Didn't kill her and no jury will say I did! They'll all be quarry workers like me or farmers who want to get back to milking their cows and don't care that there's one less Sally in Stone Valley!"

He giggled and mooed.

Jones cracked his knuckles.

* * *

"Is this a trick? I leave and you shoot me?" Pratt stepped back from the open cell door.

"Deputy Grange will drive you to the bus station," Jones told him. "Take this."

"What is it?"

"Payment. Don't return." He dropped the pouch and walked away.

"Sheriff, please, I have a book of names, important people." Nellie Porter pressed her face against the iron bars. Jones ignored her.

In an adjacent cell, George Higgins ate the egg salad sandwich Hazel had brought him.

* * *

Jones put his head on Dorcas's breast.

He could figure out most of it. On Saturday night, Higgins took the Braxton motorcar and gave Rose a ride to the Colton house where she went with him into the backyard. After he tied her up, she changed her mind and fought him. Strangled with the rope he brought, and the handkerchief found in the car, he then raped her.

Folded the clothes because he's neat? Didn't want to bother taking off her shoes and gloves? What happened to her wedding ring?

"You're still thinking about it?" Dorcas asked.

"A couple things."

"Do they matter?"

"No. I have the confession. Case closed."

"Good. Try and sleep."

He turned away from her, kept staring at the ceiling.

Hazel will make a good witness. She loves George but wants to do the right thing. She has a conscience. But even without her testimony we can convict the bastard. I have a bucket full of his lies, all about material facts regarding the murder—lies, then admissions, only because when I told him what Nellie Porter knows he couldn't squirm out of it. He and Rose were having an affair. Saturday night he was with her. I can place both in a car whose tire tracks match the ones outside the Colton backyard. Can and will.

There's no doubt now. Higgins killed her.

I'll testify to it all.

"The prosecutor will slowly swing Higgins's square knot in front of the jury."

He glanced over at Dorcas.

She kept snoring.

* * *

On the bus to Rutland, Pratt, sitting alone in the back, again counted the money. Fifty, all silver dollars.

7

Friday Day 5

Today, Shapiro had the headline and story.

ANOTHER ARREST! THE SORDID SOUTH END!
DID BUMBLING SHERIFF FINALLY GET HIS MAN?
By Lance Shapiro

In Stone Valley, a local quarryman, Roger Higgins, 32, was arrested for the brutal murder of Rose Thornton, the original suspect released from custody. Higgins was a frequent visitor to a bordello run by Mrs. Porter, a notorious madam in this small Vermont city.

Yes, it is sad to report, her home was one of ill-repute, a welcoming place for trysts and acts of debauchery. Higgins met Rose there! But sin and corruption are not limited to this brothel and the poisonous vines growing in its dark rooms that wrapped our unfortunate Rose in their twisted evil. There are other such dens of iniquity in Stone Valley, its South End a Haven for Lust.

One man is King there. Roscoe Perkins. The owner of the *Gazette*, he also collects tribute from prostitutes and the saloons where men and women sit heads bowed at the bar, not in the worship of God Almighty but their true Master—Demon Rum!

And what about our Sheriff Jones? *Did he* finally get his man or will he continue to bring out suspects one at a time like Russian nesting dolls until there isn't a last one, the real killer, small and pathetic, but none at all? The murder of Rose Thornton remaining forever unsolved!

The phone didn't ring it clamored, Jones hearing the anger. No hello, he just listened. Perkins coughed, sputtered, could barely speak, the command to appear a frenzied, short one.

In the confined, coal-burning heat of his shadow filled office, Perkins paced by having Bor rapidly push the wheelchair back and forth. Without hesitating, Jones walked in.

"He's here! Fucking Sheriff Jones! I bought cars for the whole goddamn police department and what did you come by? Mule? Keep the lid on, was that so hard to understand? Must have been because *you did the opposite! You let that Jew shine a spotlight on the whole South End and I'm its king!*"

"You wanted the murderer arrested before Sunday and I've done that," Jones stated.

Perkins's small, pink face pulsated with hate.

"Shut the fuck up! Go to the South End. Arrest that Negro. He won't get away. I've got men at roadblocks. We finish this today! Now get the fuck out, you disgust me!" He spat tobacco juice on Jones's badge.

I'll pick Dorcas up, take my furs and silver dollars, then head to Canada.

At the South End boarding house, Jones knocked on Grant's door.

"Sheriff."

"May I come in?"

Grant opened the door wider, sat on the edge of the bed. Jones used the room's one chair.

"Cigarette?"

"Thank you. Never smoked until I went into the army. When you're not fighting you talk and smoke. Or is this my last one before the firing squad?"

"Are you married, Mr. Grant?"

"I have a wife and two children, boy and girl. Abe's seven and Lucinda's four."

"How often do you see them?"

"Not as much as I'd like."

"Your work keeps you busy."

"It does."

"And that's a sacrifice you're willing to make."

"I want my son and daughter to live in a country where they can achieve according to their abilities, not be held back by the color of their skin. I want them to walk proudly, know their worth, and not bow to any man. Does that answer your question?"

"Five Negroes in Stone Valley can't be an army. Twenty or 20,000 black men with rifles won't change anything either. People will die, that's all."

"What should we do, Sheriff? Keep silent? Be grateful for crumbs?"

"Live. You can't force people to change the way they think. Powerful people make the laws. When you say equality, they hear loss, that if you have more, they'll have less. Why die for something you can't win? I'm a realist. If there isn't any game, I don't hunt."

"The privilege of a white man. What if you were black? Would *you* say yes sir, no sir, and shuffle along?"

"This isn't about color. I've made that choice many times. I'm still here. You have children. I don't. You see into the future. But our world is now, Mr. Grant. In a few years no one will remember we ever lived. Does your wife know about your militancy?"

"She knows that the only way to end suppression is to change the status quo."

"And if you die trying?"

"She will fight on and when our children are old enough, they too will join the struggle."

"One generation of death to the next."

"Until the generation after that is free. Is it time?"

"My deputies are downstairs."

Grant handed Jones an envelope.

"Will you mail this to my wife?"

"If I need to, Sergeant."

"That's the second time you've called me that. It has the sound of finality."

"This is just protective custody."

"From whom?"

"Until you can safely leave Stone Valley."

Grant nodded, and with oak-straight calmness and strength before the wind, went to the waiting policemen.

* * *

At the hotel, Shapiro nervously backed up as Jones approached him.

"I was getting ready to drive over to your office, get your side of the story. Nothing personal, Sheriff Jones." He put his hands up to protect his face.

"Let's talk."

"Good idea. Sit and talk."

They used two of the four wicker chairs placed around a piecrust table. On the staircase, in the dusky light, Jones saw men and women watching him, shadow people like those he had seen in the receiving vault. He didn't believe in ghosts. Not here, not in the cemetery, the concept of an afterlife too complex. He knew the shapes before and now were created by his mind to give death form and purpose. When they spoke, he heard himself.

Have you learned Rose's story?

Some of it.

What are you doing with this man?

"What I can…"

"I'm sorry, Sheriff, did you say something to me?"

"I wouldn't think you'd find out much down here. People coming through will talk to a reporter, but this isn't Washington or Boston. We don't have important men with interesting ideas or news staying at the Arc. The closest we had to that was a meeting held here a few years ago by big wigs in the cracker industry. Locals, and they know all the gossip, don't pay money for hotels even when they're traveling. But I have to admit, you know what you're doing. You listen, watch, creep around, then write your stories."

"I'm a reporter," Shapiro said. "That's my job."

"Writing your opinions."

"Reporting the news. I try to be fair. If I've made a mistake—"

"What you've made, Mr. Shapiro, is an enemy."

"I apologize, Sheriff, for calling you bumbling. My next story will show how clever you were in solving this difficult case."

"You decide whether I'm a fool or genius. Thank you, but I'm not the one you should worry about."

"Roscoe Perkins? Did he send you to warn me?"

"Mr. Perkins doesn't warn and he's a very dangerous man. My advice. Leave Stone Valley."

"If I don't?"

"Maybe a cracker baron out walking with his girlfriend will find your bones. Higgins lived with a woman named Hazel. He told her he murdered Rose Thornton. *That's* your next headline. Write it from Boston."

"Why are you giving me this tip?"

"It doesn't take much for people to work themselves up and form a mob. Start a rumor that a Negro assaulted a white woman and whites begin killing blacks. It happened in Atlanta, your newspaper reported it. I want Stone Valley to know about the confession, that we've arrested the murderer and he's a white man. I need that story. Perkins will print his own version hoping it lights the fuse."

"Is there a Negro in jail?"

"Just do the right thing. Send Felix a copy for the *Blade*."

"Sure thing. Thanks."

Jones got up.

"Goodbye, Mr. Shapiro. If I were you, I'd start packing."

He went hunting, tracked a bull moose that lumbered away, the fog thick and low to the ground.

Jones wondered if he could find his way back.

8

Saturday Day Six

Jones kept staring at words he could no longer see. They had become blots on a page, deformed shapes, jumbled symbols as if clotted by blood.

But he had read them—the clear, florid, deadly reporting.

Exclusive to the Phoenix!
Devil in a Dress
By Lance Shapiro

Based on my extensive investigation, this reporter located the common-law-wife of George Higgins, the man currently in custody for the murder of our Rose of Vermont.

Common- law-wife may not be an accurate description of the relationship of this woman Hazel to Higgins according to law but in every sense of the word she is his wife. They cohabited, held themselves out as husband and wife, exercised the joys of conjugal bliss. When interviewing Hazel in a boarding house owned by one Mother Mae, Hazel confided in me that Higgins, ridden with guilt and terrified of dying an unrepentant sinner, *confessed to the murder!*

The question is why.

Not why did he kill, lust can have fateful consequences, but why was Hazel putting the noose around the neck of the man she loves?

Whatever other evidence there is linking George Higgins to the crime is circumstantial, guilt or innocence becoming a jury question.

I have seen guilty men walk free and innocent men

climb to the gallows. But a confession?

That isn't the final nail in the coffin it's all of them! What was Hazel's motivation? Revenge? George, a quarry man who dresses like a dandy, did have a roving eye. The truth reveals itself in providential ways. When Hazel left the room I saw on the table beside her chair a Bible and a note sticking out from the pages. I read it, quickly jotted down the words, then put the missive back before she returned.

Here in its entirety is the message written by a woman whose Feminine handwriting we cannot reproduce but whose deceit we now expose.

My dear Pastor Thornton,
    Soon we will be together.
Love for you is my damnation.
But what worth is an immortal soul if to gain it I must live this life without you.
    I lied. Perjured myself about George. He needs me. He clings to me even more. His sickness will make me his nursemaid. Each day with him and not you is torture.
    I cannot—

The note unfinished. Was it hastily put aside when I arrived? Sin hidden in Holy Scripture! Liar! Deceiver! Corrupted scheming woman! Intending to send one Innocent Man to meet the Grim Reaper while drawing another one into her Lustful Web, the Pastor of a church who only days ago entombed his beloved wife!

But you might rightfully ask: Is Pastor Thornton so pure? Where there's smoke isn't there also fire? Yes, dear friends, as Hamlet said, That is the Question.

Tomorrow I will have more on this. The story of Rose keeps unfolding. But for now let us again speak about Truth. *A temptress is always exposed.*

At Mother Mae's, when Hazel wasn't in her room. I looked around but didn't have to look far. There they were, in a box on her desk—other love letters to the Pastor—*all unsent!*

This love affair was in her own mind... *where it should have stayed!!*

In a sidebar to Shapiro's column, one that now featured his photograph, the *Phoenix* had printed a request from Pastor Thornton:

If anyone has seen me with Hazel Higgins other than in church or by my actions or words suspect I have or had immoral relations with her report these facts and suspicions to Sheriff Jones. I call on him to investigate and make his findings public. I have nothing to hide. May God bless this troubled woman and show her mercy.

Chiles Thornton
Pastor, Stone Valley Church of Christ

Felix had reprinted Shapiro's reporting in the *Blade*, but the *Gazette* used it for another purpose.

Local Man To Be Set Free!
Negro Arrested For Murder
Of Rose Thornton

Shapiro doesn't have to worry about Bor anymore. He coordinated his story with Perkins's. Smart.

Jones squeezed his hands into tighter fists.

"Sheriff," Grange repeated. Jones looked up. "There are men outside the jail calling for Higgins to be let go. What should we do?"

"Release him. We have evidence he killed Mrs. Thornton but who will believe any of that now? When he steps out there, a free man, he's showing his ass to the law, and they'll love him for it. He's their hero, the quarry worker whose crazy wife, in cahoots with the police, tried to get him hanged. David beats Goliath again. Higgins was right. No jury will convict him."

He watched from the station's front steps as Higgins acknowledged the cheers by raising his arms over his head as if he'd just won a prize fight. Reporters took photographs, hands reached up to touch him as the surging, joyous crowd carried him toward the South End saloons.

Jones knew these men would drink and talk about protecting the purity of white women. Booze-fueled righteousness could turn them into a mob. There had never been a lynching in Vermont, but if one happened men excited by the taste of blood wouldn't just leave and go home for supper. Anarchy followed lawlessness. In the chaos, Perkins's bullyboys would guard the South End, then impose on the

North his form of order. A grateful Stone Valley would pay him. He'd have even more power.

Grant had to escape. There were two choices, car or forest.

Perkins had told him about the roadblocks, this made woodlands the better option. But avoiding getting caught in them required confusing the dogs. An athletic man might, for a few miles, stay ahead of the trackers and their hounds but if more than one group set out in search, he'd be caught unless able to hide his scent. Jones knew how, but creating multiple trails and turns required experience.

"Grange, bring your car to the back of the jail. I'll get Grant."

Unhurried, outwardly calm, Jones walked over to the jailhouse next door. When inside he immediately gave orders.

"I want four men with shotguns out front, two in the rear. *Don't shoot* but act like you will if the jail's attacked. Hold them off as long as you can. If they push forward, step aside."

Again ignoring Mrs. Porter, he unlocked Grant's cell.

"We've got to move."

Quickly inside Grange's car, they drove along a pitted roadway abandoned after construction of the mountainside passage. Jones veered sharply and accelerating through icy weeds and brambles, bounced onto the narrow mountain road.

"Perkins's boys are flatlanders. The mountains aren't for them. We might see a few tourists, that's all."

"Why are you doing this, Sheriff?"

"It's the law."

"Jim Crow or discrimination? What is the law for black people?"

"Right now, I'm only interested in one Negro who talks a lot but hasn't done anything wrong I can prove. That's why you're riding free."

"Free. After first arresting me."

"I could have let you run. You'd be dead."

"Looks like those tourists you mentioned have joined us."

Jones thought about driving straight at them, immediately knew he wouldn't get through. He stopped but kept the car running.

"Stay here."

"You remember the letter."

"I'll handle this."

Jones took his shotgun. Two of the men facing him carried rifles, two others wearing long coats held sawed-off Remingtons, the third, walking toward him, had a holstered Colt at his side.

"I don't want any trouble with you, Sheriff. Hand over the Negro and we'll all go our separate ways." Muscular, young, a jagged scar across his chin, he spoke calmly, his pale eyes showing no emotion.

"You were in the military."

"I was."

"In France?"

"That's not important."

"That man in my car, Sergeant Grant, fought in France and was decorated for bravery."

"I know who he is and what he did. But we're not fighting the Germans anymore. Our fight now is for the future of this country. Those men behind me are here because they were paid. As I did before, I've volunteered in order to kill our enemies. If I weren't with them and you were quick enough to shoot one or two, the rest would run away. I've seen that. But as you can see, I'm in command."

"Willing to die for this."

"Are you?" He took out his revolver.

"What's that nigger doing!" one of the men shouted.

Jones whirled around.

"*No!*"

Grant had backed up toward the edge of the road. A slight nod toward the sheriff then with another step backward, he fell 100 feet to the granite below.

Except for their leader, Perkins's men ran to look over the side.

"See him?'

"What's left. A smudge of black shit."

They all laughed.

"Think the old man will care?"

"Why should he?"

"He wanted a hanging."

"There's other Negroes in town."

More laughter.

"Pointless." Jones shook his head.

"Not for him or me. Men! To your cars!"

Two of the scruffy group continued staring down into the gorge, another came up and half-pushed them, the fourth drank gin from a flask. The young man fired a shot into the air.

Down the winding mountain road, crossing over to the abandoned one, a ghost road, the name fitting, Jones feeling Grant's presence in the car.

"Goddamn you." He wanted Dorcas. He wanted to sit at the bar and drink.

The crowd jeered him.

"Where is he?" a plump, soft, bookkeeper holding a new machete, called out.

Jones stopped on the police station steps.

"Here." He pointed his shotgun at the man.

The deputies unable to keep these townsmen from rushing the jail after Jones left, now closed ranks on either side of him and cocked their guns.

"On my command. Ready…"

In a few minutes all that remained of the mob were a few crushed hats, broken beer bottles, and a gleaming machete with a severed pink bookkeeper's finger dangling from the blade.

Later that night, Jones tried to save himself.

"You want my forgiveness. Disloyalty is a mortal sin and I do have the power to grant you absolution. I'm sure you understand. You were once so religious." Crimson from the burning coals coated Perkins's lips.

Hands to his sides, eyes half-closed, Bor stood in a dark corner of the office as if waiting for the command that would activate him.

"To be forgiven requires the sinner to do more than ask for it. He must admit his wrongdoing, vow never to sin again, and most importantly, humble himself. Shapiro understood that. He showed me a draft, offered it to me with pleading hands, and because what he'd written suited my purpose, I allowed him to publish it. He groveled, gave up a piece of himself, so Bor wouldn't take him for a ride. Shapiro is actually a good reporter. I look forward to working with him.

"I'll forgive you. Kneel."

Awkwardly, slowed by the weight of his heavy body, Jones dropped to his knees, his eyes at the same level as Perkins's, the old man's stare as sharp and deadly as darts dipped in poison.

"Admit your sin."

"I helped—"

"*Helped?*" Spoken with a spray of tobacco juice.

"I opened his cell and drove Grant from Stone Valley toward Rutland."

"Why?"

"To save his life."

"To defy me. You now see how stupid that was."

"Yes."

"What about your sinful nature?"

"I will do what you want."

"You already have. You gave me a dead Negro murderer! Stand reborn!" Perkins grinned, his lips pressed tightly together. "The *Gazette* will run a few stories about this agitator who murdered and raped a white woman, our saintly Rose. The reporters gone, nothing else will have changed. The South End will continue to sell pleasure, the money flowing in while Pastor Thornton mumbles in the wilderness about sin and damnation. Maybe after a year in jail and for half her profits, I'll let Nellie Porter buy back her whorehouse.

"But what about you, kneeling and pleading loyalty? How pathetic. I hate you. The town hates you. You have no future here unless I give you one and that will require more from you than words. Christ died. You need only sacrifice Dorcas."

"What has she got to do with this?"

"Nothing. That's the beauty of sacrificial atonement, you offer up the innocent, if you can call her that. Like Christ, I want you to feel pain."

"Go to hell."

"And just a moment ago you promised loyalty. Hell? You're

already there. Do you think the rocks on my hill give a shit about whether I live or die? What about the wind or the gods we create? Do they weep for us? We give meaning to the worlds we build, and my world is demanding. It's unfortunate that prostitution is such a hazardous profession. Prostitutes, even old ones, sometimes go missing and are never found.

"You'll need a reason, of course. Tell Dorcas your love for her ended when the baby died, that what you feel now when looking at her is an emptiness you can no longer pretend isn't there—something like that, use your own words. Do it and she's safe while you can go on playing sheriff.

"But sacrifice isn't devotion. Bor! Show the sheriff why he will keep loving me."

As if he were but a thin layer of scarred flesh stretched over iron bones designed to crush anything in its path, the giant marched forward on a collision course toward Jones, stopping only on Perkins's command. He handed the sheriff a slip of paper with an attachment.

I paid sheerif Jones fefty dolars to let me go.
I am stil here

The note which is the subject of this authentication was found January 11, 1919, in the cell of Asa Grant at the Stone Valley Jail. Attested to by the undersigned this 11th day of January in the year of our Lord, 1919.

Felix Henderson

Felix Henderson, AP Reporter for the *Blade* (International) Newspaper

"Like the spelling, Sheriff? It's just the way people think Negroes write. Cross me again and for a month, I'll run front-page headlines about the bribe, every story adding more details. It's so believable. Why else would a white sheriff free a black murderer. If you're lucky, you'll go to prison. Most likely, those good citizens you cheated by taking away their fun will find it again by hanging you. *That's* divine justice!

"You have until tomorrow to tell her. That's always been our deadline. Right, Bor?"

Like a trained circus animal, Bor stomped his foot.

"If you run, Jones, you and she won't get far."

In shadows, the hulking man again banged the floor.

* * *

They were in bed, looking at each other, but hadn't made love.

"Is it true, what he told you to say?"

"An emptiness? Yes, but not because of our daughter, and it has nothing to do with you. It's always been a part of my life, sometimes stronger, sometimes almost gone."

"When you're with me, what do you feel?"

"The quiet," Jones answered.

"Is that enough?"

"It was."

Dorcas closed her eyes, shutting out the light.

At the station, he gave her money and a neatly tied bundle of pelts. She lightly touched his face, boarded the train that would take her to White River Junction then, on the Central Vermont Railway, to Montreal.

Dorcas looked out the window. Jones had already left.

Back at the *Queen's End*, he drank and stared into the mirror at the bar.

9

Sunday Day Seven

The newspapers had solved the case. Asa Grant, a Negro, had raped and murdered Rose Thornton, wife of Chiles Thornton, pastor of the Stone Valley Church of Christ, and mother of three innocent Christian children.

Jones thought about Hazel.

She lied about Higgins's confession to free herself so she could turn her imaginary love affair with Thornton from ink and paper into blood and flesh. I've known women who fixated over men they couldn't have and tried to change that unpleasant fact. They schemed and fabricated, sometimes killed themselves, sometimes murdered.

But knowing that the discovery of those letters would prove she lied about the confession, why did she hide them in such obvious places?

It's as if she wanted Shapiro to find them.

* * *

"She could have stayed," Mother Mae stated. "I'm not like the others in town. I've seen what men do to women, the hurt and pain they cause. I don't know George Higgins, but Hazel seemed a sweet soul and I don't think this Pastor Thornton is as righteous as he claims.

"She packed her small suitcase and left about a half-hour ago. Poor thing. Didn't have much to show for those years she spent with him, but that's the way it is. Men control the world. That'll change. We now have the vote."

"Do you know where she was going?" Jones asked.

"To the bus. Said she had family in New Hampshire."

Stone Valley had two motor coaches, one connecting the city to Northfield, Rutland, and the towns in between, the other long distance service to Concord and Manchester, New Hampshire, then Boston.

At a small wood building not far from the railroad terminal, Jones parked beside the only bus in the lot, the interstate one, its extended body bolted onto a truck chassis.

Inside the station, two rows of five seats had waiting passengers, two men sat on the floor, in the third row Hazel sat alone.

She watched Jones walk over.

"Are you here to arrest me?"

"No." He saw the stares. "Why don't we go outside."

The day frigid and bright, their breath rising in misty clouds, they stood by the bus.

"Mrs. Thornton is dead and so is an innocent man. You'll leave and go on with your life. You spoke to me about your conscience. Maybe now you should tell me the truth about those letters. Did you hide them?"

"Not very well."

"Who were they for?

"As it turned out, Mr. Shapiro."

"When you bumped into me at the pastor's house you brought food with your name on it. Was that a love letter *I* was supposed to see?"

"Pastor Thornton has always appreciated my meat pies."

"What if instead of hiding your love for him you wanted people to know. How would it benefit you to become in the eyes of the town a crazy, treacherous woman?"

"It wouldn't. The more I'm hated, the more Mr. Higgins is loved. They're boarding."

Hazel took her suitcase and got in line. When the bus pulled away, Jones saw her sitting in back and looking straight ahead.

Jones believed he'd learned her secret. Behind those grey-blue eyes, her blonde ringlets and pale skin, sacrificial blood flowed cold.

Did George Higgins kill Rose Thornton?

The fog returned.

* * *

He could see it clearly.

When Bor answers the door, I'll drop down and use my skinning knife to slice through his left Achilles tendon. He'll scream silently and hobble after me.

In his office, I'll push Perkins out of his wheelchair, knock the oil lamp over, and when Bor enters the room, light a match.

I'll lock them both in.

What caused the fire?

A spark from the fireplace or a short in the hanging chandelier. No one will care.

I have money.

I'll get Dorcas and we'll drive South where it's warm.

Buy a boat.

Adopt.

There is justice.

I just have to wait for the right time.

* * *

Grange sat with his dolls, watched them twitch, snap their eyes and mouths open and shut.

"It's time to put Nora away," his mother said.

"But I love her."

"And hate her too. She left you."

"But I remember. We were at school, going through separate doors, and some boy pushed me. She looked over and smiled at me! In class the teacher caught me playing with a tin soldier, yanked me up by the ear, and put a dunce cap on my head. Everyone laughed but Nora.

"At lunch, I wanted to run home to the farm, maybe find a cold biscuit and some gravy—you weren't around then like you are now—but she stopped me.

'Let's sit under a tree. I have cheese, sausage, and buttermilk pie.'

She took my hand.

"She had a freckled face and wore her blonde hair in a long braid. Her pinafore was starchy and white, my overalls all muddy. That wasn't your fault. I was always clumsy. She cut her lunch into equal parts.

"The boys in school were always mean to me.

"'Look! Tub-of-Guts is sitting with a girl!' one of them yelled. She jumped up and ran after him with a stick! I was sniffling and crying. She gave me a hanky with little roses on it. She asked me if I'd like to see her drawing. It was just a bunch of bright colors and lines. She told me they were flowers and bodies telling a story. What story? I asked. Whatever you hear, she answered.

"Nora said she was going to be a famous artist. I said I was going to make sure I didn't use up all my air like my dad who got bad lungs from working in a quarry, bought a farm, then stopped beathing.

"She told me to eat my pie. That was a special day."

"She's gone. I'm still here," his mother said, her voice inside his head.

"We climbed trees together! Fished, played tag, laughed and ran. She had a lot of boyfriends."

"See. That's what I mean."

"Roscoe Perkins began buying her paintings. He moved her into his mansion."

"You had nothing to offer."

"I followed your advice. Quit any job that made me sweat."

"Because you're fat and lazy."

Grange sniffled, blew his nose in Nora's handkerchief.

"That gallery owner from Boston wanted to show Nora's work. She was going with him, but Perkins found out. Bor beat the man up, broke her fingers. Perkins heated his office by burning her paintings."

"She could have married you. You worked. Sheriff Jones had made you a deputy. Instead, she became a whore."

"Dolls get broken, mother. Sometimes you can't fix them. She died. I was with her."

"How close?"

"I don't remember. She had a painting left."

"I know. A little boy sitting under a tree. Looking at it makes me sick. You did do one thing right."

"Timed that wagon so it rolled in front of Perkin's carriage. Crippled the bastard."

"Worth the sweat, I'll give you that. I always wondered, son, why the law? So you had a reason to be in the South End? Follow her? Drive around there now? You have the box. Drop Nora in it."

"Not yet," he answered without speaking.

Grange continued offering prostitutes rides on Saturday nights. At home, and in his room of dolls, he'd sit holding the Nora one, her dirty rose embroidered handkerchief pressed tightly over her face.

10

A Month Before The Murder

"I want a divorce."

Rose and Pastor Thornton sat in their parlor, Thornton in his armchair, Rose across from him on the sofa.

"Impossible," he answered. "We are husband and wife and that, in the eyes of God, is what we will always be."

"Then God is a fool."

"Blasphemer," Thornton said without raising his voice.

"Our marriage was a fraud from the beginning. It was never consummated."

"No one will believe that. We have children."

"*I* had them. The South End served your purpose."

"I realized you have a lustful nature. You enjoy carnality."

"In all manner and fashion. It makes me feel alive. With you, I am untouched and dead."

"That's why our arrangement is mutually beneficial."

"You hide behind it."

"As do you."

"You can divorce me because I'll admit I'm an adulteress."

"Judge Wheeler will give me custody of our daughters."

"They're not yours. You wouldn't want the responsibility."

"You're right."

"Then file."

"Have you found another man?'

"Another? That's laughable. Is it necessary to discuss your hypocrisy, what I really know about you?"

She stood, crossed the floor and looked down at him.

"You have until Saturday to decide. If you don't proceed, I will. Make the right decision, that way, on Sunday, you can face your congregation confident of their continued love and respect for you. As for your God, that will always be another matter."

"Let's spend our last Christmas and New Years together as a family. We should do that for the children. January 5th you'll get your wish."

"Agreed. All neat and tidy, just the way you like things."

After she left, Thornton called George Higgins. They met in the church vestry.

"I want you to kill my wife."

"Murder Rose?"

"She's determined to divorce me. I can't have her disclosing details about our marriage. She goes to Nellie Porter's on Saturday nights. You'll need to become friends with Rose, gain her trust, engage her in frequent and various acts of physical intimacy. I know that will be difficult for you."

"I've always done what's needed."

"Will Hazel help us?"

"If I ask her."

"Most likely she'll have to leave Stone Valley. Give her this." Thornton handed Higgins an envelope. "Three hundred dollars. It'll help her get started in a new place."

"The doctor told me…"

"He isn't God," Thornton said gently. "Only the Lord knows the day and hour. I have lived my life in His service. His mercy will deliver us from judgment and grant us time."

He explained the plan.

11

The Morning After The Murder

Sunday, 1:30 am.

Having quietly left his house, Pastor Thornton walked up Summer to Winter Street and in the frozen Colton garden stood above the body of his wife, the handkerchief Higgins had used still twisted around her neck.

"You came into this world naked and cursed and that is how you will leave it."

He stripped her, tearing only the bloomers, left on shoes and gloves, the birthday gifts he'd spent time looking for and knew she would like.

"You defiled our marriage."

Thornton pulled off her wedding ring and angrily rolled the body over.

"I am a man!"

When finished, he spat on her back, then neatly folded her clothes.

Rigid, black, wrapped in moonlight and fog, Thornton strolled home while crunching on the rock candy his wife had bought for her daughters.

12

When the war ended and returning servicemen wanted clothes with a tailored look and brighter colors, always fashionable Ambrose Peabody, chief accountant for the United States Molasses Company, stopped wearing long, dark, baggy suits and began stuffing his plump body into lilac purple or sky-blue double-breasted jackets, his thick legs bulges in the matching narrow trousers.

This well cut, military influenced style was as close as Peabody ever got to wearing a uniform. During the war the draft board left him at his corporate desk. Molasses combined with water and ammonium nitrate made an explosive. Someone who could neatly write numbers in the ledger books of a molasses manufacturer was too valuable a person to lose in the muck and blood of a trench.

Arched eyebrows, puffy eyes, his hair parted down the middle and oiled so heavily that even if he had opened his large window high above a crowded North Boston Street, no stray breeze would have moved any of his carefully arranged strands.

But not only did he keep his window closed regardless of the weather, he covered it with heavy dark drapes. He hated North Boston.

Peabody heard only noise from the street below.

Another invasion larger than the last, these people Italian! They live in tenements and crowd the streets, taking over with their pushcarts, wagons, horses and stores. You can't walk two feet without seeing a grocery store or butcher shop. How many cobblers, dressmakers, and barbers do they need? What do they do with all that olive oil? Drink it? The shop owners stand outside, watching me walk past. I'm the foreigner!

Men with bushy mustaches and women carrying baskets on their head, even their hoop-rolling, hooligan children smell like garlic!

"Worse than the Irish." He pressed his laundered pocket handkerchief to his nose and cursed knowing he'd never again work in the company's Back Bay corporate office. Four years ago, the U.S. Molasses's director of distribution made him responsible for supervising the building and maintenance of The Tank.

"You're perfect for the job, Peabody. We want it built cheaply and on time."

And it was, Ambrose Peabody, who had no engineering or architectural training, able to offset his lack of knowledge by energetically doing what he knew best. He saved costs, the fifty-foot high and ninety-foot-wide storage tank holding over two million gallons of molasses, built with thin metal walls and less rivets than needed.

The Tank's colossal size cast a shadow over the buildings in Boston's North End.

"Excuse me, sir." The man stood hat-in-hand at the office door.

Peabody quickly put the handkerchief down.

"Yes? What is it?"

"I hate to bother you, sir—"

"Hate to, but you are."

"The neighbors. They say the tank is leaking."

"Then fix it. That's your job."

"I—uh—"

"Not capable? Maybe I should hire a handyman who is. It's probably just some seepage. These people are always bellyaching about something. Give their children sticks and tell them they can have all the molasses they scrape off the sides."

"I don't know for sure—"

"Which means you do." Peabody glared at him, the workman stepping back.

"Some of the leaks, if there are any, might be… high."

"But not high enough. Get a ladder and grey paint. Cover them up. If no one sees them no one will complain."

Peabody took his pen from its inkstand and went back to writing perfectly formed numbers in a column of them.

After work, on his way to the overhead train, he glanced around and thought about splashing ink on the sign of a new business advertising homemade macaroni and spaghetti but decided instead to kick a pebble at the door. A wool scarf hiding his face, he quickly walked away.

The street deserted, the moon only a sliver of light, Peabody thought he heard footsteps behind him.

The spaghetti man? With a knife?

Sweating, hunched over, he ran, The Tank, looming in front of him, rumbling from deep within its molasses belly. His pants split, his stomach flopped below his vest, and his hair unraveled.

Breathing hard, he stopped, and bending over, held his sides.

Silence. No footsteps. No grumbling metal.

"Damn that man. Leaks my ass. I'm firing him tomorrow."

Peabody pulled his hair back in shape, adjusted his suit, and enjoying the quiet and emptiness, walked briskly to the station.

13
January 14-15

Thornton drove, Higgins took the bus. They checked into separate rooms in a Boston North End hotel. Both men needed a few days' vacation. They ate lunch together, visited historical sites, and enjoyed a candlelight dinner in Thornton's suite. The pastor told Higgins if he wanted ice cream for dessert he should first try finishing his steak.

They slept peacefully and late. After breakfast in bed, the men dressed and left the room.

The weather warmer than it had been the previous days, people bustled about enjoying the sunshine. Vendors sold, women bought meat and fresh vegetables, children played in the street.

"You need a haircut," Prescott remarked.

"I'm not cutting it short, don't even ask!"

"You look common."

"I am." Higgins smiled.

"No sense advertising it. When we're done here, I'll buy you a new suit. Not something I'd wear—"

"I hope not, mister dark and gloomy!" Higgins puckering his lips and sounding like a child.

About to enter the barbershop, they heard a roar, a thunderclap, the staccato sound of rivets shooting into the air as the molasses tank exploded, shaking the ground.

At 12:30am, a 25-foot wave of thick syrup rolling forward bent the steel girders of the elevated railroad train, toppled streetcars, knocked small buildings over, and buried everything in its path.

Crushed by the horse falling on him, Higgins died gasping for air. He'd almost reached Thornton's hand sticking up through the molasses, the rest of the pastor submerged, head down.

Ambrose Peabody escaped and a day later was transferred to the company's home office.

Epilogue

Roscoe Perkins died in his sleep.

Sheriff Jones attended the funeral and stood beside Bor, who, with his mouth stretched wide, expelled through this dark, cavernous opening, only air as he tried forcing the sound of grief from his silenced voice.

Jones threw dirt on the coffin.

Nellie Porter became Boss of the prosperous and growing South End, its new buildings, sidewalks, streetlamps, and bright lights, paid for by what this part of town had always sold—alcohol and women. Unchanged too was collection Sunday, Sheriff Jones making the rounds for his new employer.

One night, when leaving the Perkins's abandoned mansion, he saw Bor sitting on a large rock, his head down. Jones gave him a ride to the station and let him sleep in one of the empty cells. The station became Bor's home. During the day, he stood in a corner of the sheriff's office.

Flames, their origin unknown, burned down Perkins's mansion, leaving only his fireplace and its blackened chimney that continued to melt ice and snow.

After six months trying to run the *Gazette*, Felix Henderson had bankrupted the paper by investing its profits in a company that manufactured coffins with safety bells inside. He returned to the *Blade*, wrote articles on spiritualism and a medium who spoke to her dead brother using a teleplasmic hand.

Lance Shapiro disappeared while covering the Polish-Soviet war.

* * *

At the *Queen's End*, Jones, drinking alone at the bar, knew it served no purpose to think about the other trails he might have followed. Those lives never happened. Even the path he'd chosen had vanished behind him, Dorcas and his daughter both gone. What was better? To trudge ahead toward eventual oblivion or find it now?

A woman sat down next to him.

"Buy me a drink, Sheriff?"

Why talk to her when you have that ghost costume without eyes? Put it on, boy. Be an ass.

"What would you like?" he answered.

* * *

In a thicket, not more than 150 feet away, Jones saw the old bull moose he had lost before. Slowly, he raised his rifle.

It'll hear the sound and not knowing its dead keep chewing.

The moose slowly turned its head.

Jones looked into its large dark eyes—

He kept his finger on the trigger.

* * *

Two years after Rose Thornton's murder, a newspaper boy on his early morning route, found the naked body of a woman lying face down on ice.

Acknowledgments

Thank you, Marianne, for helping edit this story.

Thank you, Grace, for bringing my manuscripts to life.